Molly Pepper
& the
Night Train

Courtney King Walker (signature)

Courtney King Walker

Lands
Atlantic
PUBLISHING

For my parents, who encouraged me to dream
and made me work even harder.

CHAPTER

1

The Real Face of Adventure

When she opened the mailbox on the first day of summer break, Molly Pepper found three pieces of mail. The first two items did not seem all that interesting: one, a Woman's Day magazine; two, her final report card on which she already knew mostly C's would be hogging all the white space; and three, a small, crème-colored envelope with her name on it.

That was the most interesting discovery. Molly could not recall the last time she had ever received anything in the mail. Not only was the crisp, smooth envelope addressed to her, but it also lacked both a return address *and* a stamp. No stamp meant somebody had sidestepped the entire mail system altogether and placed this exact letter into her mailbox, probably this very day.

Molly popped a cinnamon bear into her mouth and peered over her shoulder for any chance that the owner of the envelope might still be watching her. All she discovered behind her, however, was the sound of the distant ferry whistling through the salty air, and the passing by of an old, white convertible spewing a fume of exhaust in its wake. She coughed in protest, and then ducked behind a lone, thick palm tree, in case she was mistaken. She wasn't going to take any chances. Who knew what might be out there, hiding in the shadows, watching her every move?

For twenty-point-five seconds, Molly chewed on the remainder of cinnamon goo in her mouth and held her position while surveying the neighborhood for any sign of bedlam.

But, she hated to admit; everything appeared just as it should.

Same as always.

With a sigh, Molly tucked her report card into her back pocket for safekeeping and reemerged from behind the palm tree, doing her best to appear carefree. But it was more difficult than she'd hoped, especially after her detour to the side of the house where she deposited the

Woman's Day magazine into the recycle bin.

Secretly stashing unwanted mail had been her routine for the last few months. She'd taken it upon herself to bury any rogue reminders of her mother under a pile of crumpled newspapers before her dad ever had a chance to see them. Molly figured it was better she deal with the mess of their new life than him. Especially today, the first day of summer break that was *supposed* to be filled with the promise of adventure...not reminders of broken promises.

The house was quiet when Molly stepped inside, except for the sound of her dad's daytime snores flooding the hallways like an occasional blast of an off-tune trombone.

That sound this time of morning always put Molly in a despondent mood because it meant *change*—an unwanted, unrequested change she hadn't yet grown used to. Secretly, she wished her dad would learn how to sleep in silence. Then, she could live under the ruse that her life remained the same as last summer when the world was still the kind of place in which most people liked to stay put.

At the kitchen table, Molly pushed aside yesterday's mail to make room for the letter. *Her* letter.

Now, the moment of truth. She hesitated

before opening it, trying to guess just what it could be...a note from a secret admirer? A party invitation? *Russian correspondence?*

She sucked in a deep, audible breath. Then, on the count of three she exhaled and popped open the pointed flap.

A thick, crème-colored note slipped out onto the table, revealing a simple sentence printed in black ink, each line spaced evenly from top to bottom.

**IF ADVENTURE
IS YOUR DESIRE
GO TO
174 CANDLESTICK HILL
AT NINE O'CLOCK TONIGHT
NO SOONER
NO LATER**

Well. There wasn't a question in Molly's mind about her desire for adventure. In fact, if anybody desired adventure more than her, she would like to meet them face-to-face just to see what the *real* face of adventure looked like. Because she was pretty sure the freckled face she met in the mirror each morning silently begged for something more than this—more than entertaining herself all summer long while her father worked two shifts at the police department and slept it off the next morning.

Adventure was the *easy* part.

The *difficulty* about this whole message, if Molly chose to follow the card's directions after all (and she was definitely still debating the whole idea), was the getting-to-the-top-of-Candlestick-Hill-without-passing-out part.

See, Candlestick Hill was the steepest hill in all of California. In fact, if Blue Rock Island were situated a little closer to Canada instead of in the middle of the San Francisco Bay, Candlestick Hill would make the world's best ski run. But, a thick blanket of fog was as close to white the island ever got, making Candlestick Hill a nightmare instead of the attraction it could be.

Therefore, a little skepticism about the mysterious message was in order. The more Molly thought about it, the more she wondered if perhaps somebody was playing a joke on her just to get her to climb the murderous hill for nothing.

Who would do something like that?

Molly chewed on that thought along with another cinnamon bear, and drummed her fingers along the tabletop, trying to come up with a few criteria. First off, somebody with easy access to her mailbox; secondly, somebody creative enough to make up the whole idea in the first place; and lastly but most importantly, somebody who knew Molly well enough to play on her longing for adventure.

Somebody probably like...

"What's that?" asked a voice coming from a space right behind her.

Molly coughed on her cinnamon bear and whirled around as the beginning of a scream eked its way out of her throat. She stopped just before it grew loud enough to wake her dad. "Noah!" Molly hit her next-door neighbor on the arm. "Why are you sneaking up on me?"

"I'm not. You didn't answer when I knocked, and I know your dad's rule about ringing the doorbell, so..."

"You could have warned me! I thought you were a burglar."

Noah Wonderly rubbed his arm and pulled out a chair beside Molly. "I'm sorry. But, I *did* knock, you know."

Molly slid the mysterious note across the table. "Do you have any idea what this is?" she asked, getting right down to business.

She wanted to gauge Noah's reaction, certain if he were behind it, the truth would reveal itself immediately. He could never withhold information without the whole truth bleeding out through his shifty brown eyes and seesawing smile. Because of that, Noah was a terrible secret-keeper and an even worse actor.

When they were kids, Noah was the lousiest performer in the history of neighborhood plays, resulting in Molly having to play both Darth Vader *and* Princess Leia (which didn't turn out so well). Even now, Molly could tell by the way Noah shifted his eyes to the right whenever they made eye contact that he had a crush on her.

But, she was careful not to let on because she wasn't quite sure how she felt about him. Not yet.

Noah picked up the crème-colored note and studied both sides of it very thoughtfully, as if taking a test. His eyes narrowed as he mouthed the words of the message quietly to himself.

Molly couldn't stand how long he took just to consider a few words on a piece of paper, and immediately concluded that he was much too serious to be part of any practical joke. She snatched the note back from him, a little relieved.

"Is it some kind of joke?" he asked, helping himself to the bag of cinnamon bears lying open on the table. She allowed it.

"I thought the same thing," she said, glad she wasn't the only one to jump to conclusions.

"Who's it from?"

"I don't know. I found it in the mailbox."

Noah glanced at the note. "Well, are you going to go up there tonight?"

Molly thought for a minute, but still didn't know what her answer should be. She wanted to go. The promise of adventure had definitely piqued her interest. But, at the same time, she felt this deep, lurking fear building up inside her. What if she went all the way up there, only to be met with...*nothing?*

"Not sure," Molly said. "I have to think about it for a little while. I'm trying to decide if it will even be worth the climb."

"I don't think you should go."

She looked up, surprised. "Why not?"

"I just don't trust it," he said, revealing a bit of the blood-red remains of his demolished cinnamon bear. "What if it really is a joke?"

Molly sunk back into her chair, not sure what she should do. She had hoped for a little more support from him than this.

Noah remained quiet, his mind searching for a solution, a way to help Molly without her having to risk falling victim to some kind of mischief. Noah Wonderly was that kind of friend—the kind to back you up when you didn't know where to go next, and the kind to offer up solutions to problems that weren't even his. Molly almost always felt happier when he was around; he had his own way of making everything look brighter, even on a foggy day. San Francisco had a lot of foggy days.

And he also *usually* smelled like a clean laundry room.

Though, that didn't mean Molly *liked* Noah, or anything.

"What about your dad? Would he drive you up and check it out for you?" Noah asked, dropping his chin on his hands.

"Nope. He'll be at work. Plus, policemen don't approve of this kind of correspondence."

"You mean, like secret messages?"

"Yes. Secret messages. Not exactly a police-approved activity. We'll have to keep this one under wraps. Which means if my dad starts asking questions, you'd better leave. He'll be able to tell you're hiding something just by looking at you."

"What? No he won't!" Noah jerked upright and ran his hands through his dark hair, as if proving he was smooth and had skills.

Molly pointed a finger. "That look on your face right now...*guilty*."

"What are you talking about?" A hesitant smile spread across Noah's face, despite his every effort to tame it.

Molly laughed.

"What's so funny?" asked Noah, laughing now, too, though he wasn't sure what he was even laughing about. But, that was the thing about Molly, and the whole reason he liked her. Everything about Molly Pepper was contagious, making it that much harder to be around her when she was sad.

Molly looked up at him. "If I decide to go, will you come with me?"

Noah wasn't sure about that. Did he want to go? Not really—who wanted to climb Candlestick Hill *ever?* Plus, he wasn't very excited about chasing after an anonymous prankster. It just seemed…stupid, and maybe even a little bit dangerous.

On the flipside, he never turned down an opportunity to hang out with Molly, especially when it meant the chance to prove he was brave and strong and all that other macho stuff girls liked. What guy wouldn't want that?

But, first, he thought he might as well ring in a favor in exchange, and hoped Molly wouldn't run away screaming at his request. Especially when she found out there might be spiders involved. "Yes," he said with his shifty eyes. "But I need you to help me with something, first."

CHAPTER

2

The car backfired when it pulled into the neighborhood, which was the last thing Ruby Dodd wanted to happen seeing as how she was supposed to be undercover.

Why the bureau didn't give her something a little more inconspicuous, maybe something made in *this* decade instead of the one in which she was born, was beyond her. But, she had a job to do, and complaining about vehicle options was not it.

The ferry ride over had been uneventful, just like every other day for the past month. Although, this morning Ruby couldn't figure out how the ferry captain could see through the fog enough to land safely on Blue Rock Island instead of crashing into the rocks at the base of the Golden Gate Bridge.

She was relieved when they docked right on time at ten am. The drive to Penny Lane was a mere five minutes, and she parked in her usual spot around the corner from the stucco rambler, close enough to see the front of the house...but not so close that she would be spotted.

Ruby eyed her watch and started counting down. She had a feeling something would happen today. It was June 13th, Moody's five-year anniversary. Just thinking about it made her exhausted—five years of following clues all leading to dead-ends.

Until now.

She was this close. *This close!*

At the thought of victory, Ruby smiled, until a UPS deliveryman wearing brown shorts and a brown shirt emerged from the fog. She sat up straight in her seat when he stopped in front of the small, stucco house and placed something the size of a letter inside the mailbox.

Ruby looked around for any sign of his truck. Certainly he had other packages to deliver? But, just as she suspected, the UPS man walked to the end of the street, turned the corner, and disappeared. The fog seemed to blot out his existence.

Ruby panicked. She didn't know whether to

chase after the man or try to intercept the correspondence inside the mailbox before it was discovered.

She jumped out of her car, ready to spring to action, but stopped at the sight of Molly Pepper already standing in front of the mailbox, peering inside.

Shoot!

Now it was too late. The UPS man had vanished, and Molly Pepper had already found his message.

That left Ruby with no other choice. Today she would follow that girl's every move.

CHAPTER

3

Three Feet Under

They stood together in Noah's front entryway while Molly marveled at the size of the chandelier suspended from the twenty-foot ceiling.

She could never quite get over the fact that the Wonderlys lived like kings here in their two-story beach house next door to Molly's modest rambler. But, *somebody* had to have the biggest house on the street, and *somebody else* had to have the smallest; those two somebodies just usually didn't live right next to each other.

"So, what's this all about?" Molly asked, referring to Noah's request for her help with something he'd called, "goal number three."

"I need you to be my witness," Noah's voice echoed through the entryway and disappeared down the empty hall like a fleeing ghost.

"Like, as a witness to a crime? You're not planning on killing someone, are you?"

Noah rolled his eyes. "Can you get serious for one minute? I'm talking about a goal I made. Remember my goal list?"

"You don't play soccer," Molly said, trying not to laugh at her joke.

"Not a soccer GOAL. Will you just focus for one second?"

"*What* goal, Noah?"

"Don't you remember? Two weeks ago I showed you my list of goals for the summer, and you laughed and said, 'who makes goals for summer?' Remember that?"

The moment came rushing back. Molly *did* remember laughing at Noah's five-item-long list printed on a crinkly piece of lined paper. "Oh, right. Got you. What was on it, anyway? I can't remember the details."

"That's what I'm talking about. I've already made it to number three. And now I need you to be my witness to prove I did it."

"Number *three?*" Molly asked. "What were numbers one and two on your list, and why didn't I get to witness those?"

"They were easy ones. Number one was to sit through 'I Am Legend' without covering my eyes or screaming once. My mom was my witness there. And, number two was to do fifty pushups and sit-ups every morning before breakfast for two weeks straight. I figured I wouldn't need a witness for that because, well, isn't it obvious? You can actually *see* the results of my hard work now." Noah stepped backward and lifted his shirt to reveal a very skinny, very pale belly. "Pretty impressive, huh?"

"Yeah. Sure. Put your shirt down."

"Anyway. Number three is a little trickier. I need you to watch me go down into the crawl space beneath my house."

"Why would you want to do that?" Molly asked. "There are…like…bugs and mice and dead bodies down there."

"I *have* to do it. Small, dark spaces terrify me."

"That didn't answer my question AT ALL. I repeat: Why would you ever *want* to do that? ESPECIALLY if you're scared of small, dark spaces?"

"My dad says if I want to stop being a wimp, I need to face my fears. So that's what I'm trying to do—facing my fear of small, dark spaces," Noah explained.

"That doesn't make any sense. I'm scared of murderers, but you don't find me chasing after them, do you?"

"That's not the same thing." Noah rolled his eyes again, a hint of impatience showing through. "Plus, my mom always leaves some kind of surprise message for me after I complete my goal. It's kind of fun to look for."

"What kind of message?"

"I don't know. Just something encouraging."

"I guess that's kind of cool. I suppose if you need that kind of motivation, then...well...whatever." Molly suddenly felt uncomfortable, though she wasn't sure why— other than for the fact that maybe, possibly, she was a little bit jealous Noah's mom made such a big deal about stupid goals.

In some needy way, Molly wished her dad did something like that, too.

"I just need you to hold the flashlight and count to ten for me. Oh, and also make sure I come back up. That's the most important thing."

Noah's eyes transitioned from impatient to frightened, and Molly noticed.

"Okay. I'll do it," she agreed, though reluctantly. "Just promise me you'll come right up if you see any dead bodies. And if you see a spider, I don't want to hear about it. Got it?"

Noah agreed and led her down the hallway and into his parents' bedroom. Mr. Wonderly was at work, and Noah's mom was currently in the kitchen whipping up one of her fancy desserts as usual, while Noah's older sister, Sarah, was off on a babysitting job. That left the front part of the house empty, giving Molly and Noah plenty of breathing room.

The Wonderly's closet rivaled the size of Molly's kitchen. Tucked under the front staircase, it made for multiple levels of ceilings angling this way and that, giving Molly the impression of being stuffed into the upper floor of a dollhouse where the furniture no longer fit and the dolls' heads bumped into the roof.

In the far corner of the closet, Noah dropped to his knees. Molly crouched beside him as he peeled back the carpet.

"Hold the flashlight," he ordered.

Molly shined the flashlight just over his head. The dim, shaky light caught the top of his fingers as he lifted a trapdoor hidden under a corner of carpet.

They stared down into a dark, musty hole. It smelled of damp, dark soil, laden with the essence of something forbidden.

Noah nudged Molly. She wondered why he was shaking. "This is where I go down," he said quietly.

"Really? That's the plan? Just hop right down beneath the house?"

He nodded his head, yes.

"But, what if there's a skeleton down there…or worse, a bunch of spiders?"

Noah gulped, and then lowered himself backwards into the hole. "I'm not scared. I can do this," he whispered more to himself than to her.

Molly decided to chime in, too, as she was there specifically for moral support. "You can do this," she said, shining the flashlight in his face until his entire head took on a ghoulish cast, like a zombie filled with blood.

"I have to stay under for two minutes."

"WHAT?" Molly yelled. "What kind of dumb-crazy goal is that?"

Noah ignored her. "Are you ready? Close the door and count to one hundred and twenty as soon as I'm all the way under, okay?"

"When–"

"NOW!"

Smack. The door was down.

"ONE. TWO. THREE. FOUR. FIVE. SIX. SEVEN. EIGHT. NINE. TEN. ELEVEN. TWELVE. THIRTEEN. FOURTEEN. FIFTEEN. SIX—"

Molly sensed sudden movement behind her. She spun around and shined the flashlight out into the Wonderly's dark bedroom. "Hello?" she called.

The door creaked. Molly aimed the flashlight above and around her until the tip of a fluffy grey tail swooshed by. She relaxed, grateful it was only Noah's cat.

The hard, repetitive sound of banging echoed through the trapdoor. Molly spun back around, certain she could hear a muffled scream. She lowered her head closer to the trapdoor, trying to listen.

"Let me out of here!" Noah's voice pleaded through the boards.

"But, you said—"

"NOW!"

Molly lifted the trapdoor. Up popped Noah's head, his hair covered in cobwebs, and two long smudges of dirt crawling up his cheeks.

"What happened?" she asked, afraid for the answer.

Without a single word, he pulled himself out of the opening and swiped the flashlight out of Molly's hands.

"But—"

"Come on," he said, stomping the trap door shut and kicking the carpet into place. "I can't do it. Not today."

Molly felt a little melancholy as she watched

Noah storm out of the closet, his head lowered and shoulders hunched. He was usually the one to cheer her up, to brighten her dark mood. This wasn't right—not right *at all*.

At that, a delicious thought entered her brain. She jumped to her feet and ran out the door with the perfect suggestion to distract Noah from his failed attempt, and to hopefully brighten his mood.

CHAPTER

4

The Sweeter Side of Blue Rock Island

The fog lifted just in time for a ride into town. Blue Rock Island was mainly flat—just small enough to travel from one side to the other on foot or bicycle without much effort. Well, except for Candlestick Hill and the rocky cliffs on the east side of the island. But, nobody ever ventured over there; Bell's Bluff—the old, abandoned prison at the end of the gated road was enough of a deterrent for sane people.

After a ten-minute ride across town, Molly and Noah secured their bicycles in the bike rack by the front door of *Flaky's Fantastic Doughnuts*, the best and only doughnut shop on the island.

Inside, it smelled of fried fat and buttery

sugar, Molly's favorite scent since the day *Flaky's Fantastic Doughnuts* opened a little over six months ago. She looked around the shop. Two other customers shared a small table; other than them, Molly and Noah seemed to have the rest of the place to themselves. Molly's stomach growled at the sight of chocolate, glaze and sprinkles neatly lined up inside the lighted glass case.

A door behind the counter swung toward them, and Molly looked up. Out walked a tall, muscular man with white hair and thick arms. "May I help yo...*Molly!*" he exclaimed the instant his eyes rested upon his newest customers. "What brings you here this morning?"

Molly laughed. It was the same question Tom Flaky always asked whenever she came for a visit. As if there were a reason to visit a doughnut shop other than to satisfy a craving for doughnuts.

Before Molly could respond, Tom Flaky glanced past them, surveying the shop, and then propped the swinging door open with his foot. "Come on," he said, motioning for Molly and Noah to follow him into the back room where all the doughnut magic happened.

Soft, brassy music greeted them—an old-fashioned song with horns and percussion drums, and a smooth, jazzy singer belting out something about "flying away." It made Molly want to dance, though she kept her chin up and shoulders back in an attempt to be on her best behavior.

"It's so cool back here," Noah said above the music, voicing aloud the very thing Molly happened to be thinking.

Tom Flaky twisted a knob on the wall, and the music faded to a soft hum. "Welcome to my bakery, Miss Molly and Mr. Wonderly." Molly loved how Tom Flaky always called her 'Miss Molly.' It was what her mother called her, too. "Why don't you two find a seat?"

Along the back wall, Molly and Noah each settled onto a stool. The memory of failing at goal number three was quickly replaced by the thrill of watching Tom Flaky pound, and flip, and flour, a bowling ball-sized wad of powdery dough. Molly thought it was amazing what he could make from a regular dough ball.

Molly always looked forward to these visits once or twice a week. When she wasn't invited into the back, she would sit at her own table out front and enjoy her free doughnut in silence. Tom Flaky would come out to greet her; sometimes he might even pull up a chair while she snacked on her doughnut, and ask about her day. Eventually he'd wander back behind the counter to wait on other customers. But, before Molly left, Tom Flaky would almost always wink at her and look the other way, as if keeping a big secret.

"You might as well go ahead and make your choice," he said, looking up from his dough. "I know that's all you can think about."

That was their cue. They jumped off their stools and raced to the cooling racks. Molly scooped up an apple fritter without giving it much thought, the only relevant consideration being the apple fritter was the biggest doughnut on the shelf, and she hadn't eaten much for breakfast. Noah, on the other hand was forever standing in front of the cooling rack; he always took at least five minutes to decide, and Molly's taste buds didn't have patience for that.

In the back corner, away from all the commotion of Noah's indecision and Tom's doughnut making, Molly sat up to an empty counter. As she munched, her eyes fell on a large poster hanging on the wall, its edges peeling up at the corners. She was pretty sure she had never seen it before.

She slid off her chair for a closer look, but felt a chill shudder through her when she realized she was looking at a black and white photo of the dreaded Bell's Bluff prison. It looked like a haunted house to her—or worse, a haunted prison, its gray walls riddled with dark window holes, the whole thing covered in creature-like overgrown bushes.

Wisps of fog clinging to the corners of the prison made Molly cold just looking at it. Even worse, at the very bottom of the poster, a row of mug shots of three different Bell's Bluff convicts all seemed to glare at her from the poster, like Molly was on their most-wanted list.

All the convict stories Molly had heard over the years, about Bell's Bluff inmates committed for life for murdering children like her, jumped to the forefront of her mind. Ever since she'd chosen the dare part of *truth or dare* and had ventured to the other side of the island to see for herself the infamous prison's locked-up gate threaded with barbed wire, she'd been plagued with nightmares of Bell's Bluff and its prisoners.

To her, even after its closing, Bell's Bluff was akin to every kind of horror imaginable— especially of dying and death.

And Molly wanted nothing to do with death.

She swallowed another bite of fritter and averted her eyes, though it was hard *not* to look, knowing she was being watched.

One convict with the number 1331 glared

out from the poster with a pair of deep-set eyes and a devastatingly somber frown that made him seem almost sad. Molly wondered who this man was and what he'd done to be sent to the most terrifying prison in all of America.

"What are you doing over here?" barked a voice that had somehow crept up behind her.

Molly screamed and spun around, convinced she was about to get murdered.

CHAPTER
5

Who's Afraid of the Big, Bad Wolfe?

Only Noah and Tom Flaky stood behind her. Noah was halfway through a jelly-filled doughnut, with sticky red all over his fingers while Tom Flaky leaned against an empty cooling rack, calmly watching her, his arms folded across his apron.

To avoid explaining, Molly took another bite of fritter while Tom Flaky suggested she and Noah finish their snack out front. "It's time for me to get back to work," he said, his bushy, gray eyebrows moving up and down like a caterpillar inching along his forehead.

Noah followed Molly as she pushed through the swinging door, and immediately took a seat at the nearest table. He pulled out a dozen brown napkins from the dispenser to sop up the mess stuck all over his hands while Molly wondered how it was possible to be so overrun by a doughnut.

"My parents would die if they knew I was eating a doughnut for lunch," Noah said, in between slobbery bites of jam-filled deliciousness. He was right. Noah's parents didn't have a speck of sugar in their house, which probably explained why Noah raided Molly's cinnamon bears every chance he got. And why he looked so happy this very moment.

Molly pulled a chair out across from Noah to join him, but noticed a policeman sitting by himself at a small table near the front window. Because of her dad's job, Molly was familiar with most of Blue Rock Island's police force. But she had never seen this particular policeman before. And, she was sure she would have noticed that thick, black hair and ugly moustache sandwiched between his mouth and big, long nose.

Molly inched closer. The policeman was seconds away from taking a bite out of a glazed doughnut bursting at the seams with cream, and she wondered what would happen to all the cream once he bit down. It was certain to be an explosion.

She held her breath in anticipation.

Seconds before he would bite, the policeman

stopped and lifted his eyes until they rested directly on Molly.

Oops. She hadn't planned on being discovered. She just wanted to observe.

"Hi," he said.

"Oh, hi," Molly answered. "Is that pretty good with all the cream inside?"

"Yep."

"I'm going to have to try that next time."

He grunted something indecipherable, and Molly almost turned away, but felt something inside her go still when he spoke again. His voice was barely above a whisper, like he wanted only *her* to hear him. "Sorry to hear about your mom."

Molly was unsure how to respond. *It's okay?* (it wasn't). *Don't worry about it?* (why would *he* worry, anyway?). Not only did Molly not like people talking to her about her mother, but she especially resented it coming from a stranger.

"And what about your grandparents? Have you seen them lately?" he asked.

Molly's gaze dropped to the floor. She was not going to talk about her mother or her grandparents right now, especially not with a strange policeman with too big a moustache. She scanned the room as if searching for a lifeline, until her eyes found a spot on which to focus again—the policeman's nametag.

A-ha!

"Your name is Officer Wolfe?" Molly asked, trying to take charge by changing the subject and going on the offensive. She preferred to be the one asking all the questions.

He nodded, though at mention of his name, Officer Wolfe seemed slightly uncomfortable. *Good.* That was the plan, thought Molly as she studied him, wondering why he was talking about her mother, and about grandparents she didn't have anymore.

"You new on the force?" Molly asked, staring into his dark BB-like eyes.

He placed his untouched doughnut on his plate and wiped his fingers. "Just got transferred from San Francisco. Working on a new case," he said, almost too confidently, like Molly should be impressed.

"I see," replied Molly, wondering if her dad knew this guy. "Well, welcome to the island. And just so you know, most kids on Blue Rock Island don't talk to strangers."

Molly felt her face warming, and her pulse quickening. As she returned to her table to finish her apple fritter, she wondered why this strange policeman had asked her such personal things.

It was a sore subject, too. Only a few years ago, her dad's parents lived across the bay. She and her mom and dad would take the ferry to visit them every weekend to eat Grandma Pepper's famous sourdough pancakes. That was the last thing Molly remembered ever saying to her grandmother: "*Mmmmm, those pancakes were delicious!*" And then both of them dropped dead one morning, just like that. First her grandmother from pneumonia, and then her grandfather, who just never woke up.

Molly's grandparents on her mother's side were another story entirely. Molly had never even met them, didn't even know what they looked like because they'd both been dead a long, long time. From what she'd been told, she gathered that both her grandparents died when her mom was just a little girl. Molly's mom moved in with her aunt and uncle in San Francisco after that, and lived with them her whole life until she got married.

Molly's mom could only recall distant memories of her father, but loved to tell stories about his life as a magician. Molly had a hard time imagining such a life, but played along though, just to keep the stories coming and a smile on her mother's face.

When Molly found out her grandfather had died when her mother was only ten, Molly wondered if her mom wasn't just making it all up. "Couldn't he just use his magic and come back to life?" Molly had asked, grinning inside.

Molly's mother just shook her head despondently and replied that it wasn't that kind of magic. Only card tricks and disappearing rabbits...small sleights of the hand like that. "Illusions," she'd said, as if that explained everything.

Officer Wolfe's questions about her grandparents had squelched Molly's appetite. Suddenly, she didn't care anymore about Officer Wolfe or his seam-splitting doughnut. She was ready to go home now, despite the unfinished apple fritter soaking through a napkin on the table.

Officer Wolfe had ruined Molly's doughnut outing.

Reluctantly, she dumped her fritter in the trashcan and waited at the front door for Noah to finish cleaning up his doughnut mess. She deliberately turned her back on Officer Wolfe so she wouldn't have to look at him anymore.

That was when she noticed an eye-catching advertisement taped up on the wall—one that she couldn't ignore. It was printed in black and white, with a small illustration of a train at the very top.

Molly stepped closer.

**THE NIGHT TRAIN
EXPECT THE UNEXPECTED.
IMAGINE THE UNIMAGINABLE.
BELIEVE THE UNBELIEVABLE.**

DON'T MISS YOUR CHANCE FOR A ONE-OF-A-KIND ADVENTURE ON BLUE ROCK ISLAND'S NIGHT TRAIN ON JUNE 13TH.

50 LUCKY WINNERS WILL BE RANDOMLY SELECTED TO EXPERIENCE THE MOST OUTRAGEOUS RIDE THIS SIDE OF THE GOLDEN GATE.

TO BE ENTERED INTO A DRAWING FOR A CHANCE AT WINNING YOUR VERY OWN NIGHT TRAIN TICKET, PLEASE VISIT OUR WEBSITE AT WWW.THENIGHTTRAIN.COM BEFORE MIDNIGHT ON THE FIRST DAY OF JUNE.

LOTTERY TICKETS ARE $100 EACH.

WINNERS' INVITATION AND INSTRUCTIONS WILL BE DELIVERED ON OR BEFORE THE 13TH.

GOOD WIT!
(BECAUSE LUCK IS FOR CRIMINALS).

"Noah. What's the date?" Molly asked.

He looked at his watch. "June thirteenth."

June thirteenth… That was tonight!—the actual night for the Night Train adventure… *supposedly.*

But, even though she loved the idea of the unexpected, unimaginable and unbelievable, Molly couldn't help being skeptical about the whole thing. Sure, when she first saw the ads popping up around the island six months ago, it was the only thing she could think about. Everyone at her middle school had talked about it like it was the coolest, most secret thing ever.

Now, however, Molly felt she was too old for "believing the unbelievable."

Noah came up behind her. "Do you think the Night Train is even *legit?*" he asked.

"I used to. But now I think it's just a scam."

"Why?"

"Name one person who's actually even seen a train on our island."

Noah lifted his eyes and searched the ceiling above, as if really giving it some thought. But, just as Molly suspected, he was unable to name a single person.

"That doesn't mean anything," he countered. "We only know kids our age, and most kids in middle school don't have a hundred dollars to throw away in a lottery."

Molly wasn't sure what to believe. Noah *did* have a point, but Molly recalled his belief in the tooth fairy lasting much longer than it should have.

"That sure is something, isn't it?" said a deep voice behind them.

Molly and Noah spun around. Officer Wolfe stood right behind them, his body much too close to them as he, too, focused his attention on the Night Train flier.

"Never heard of such a thing in my life," he said, scratching his chin, his voice deep and raspy. "Do you believe it's even real? I've heard some people say it's just a trick. What do *you* think, Molly?"

Hearing Officer Wolfe use her name was unnerving. She was of the belief that there had to be some sort of unspoken agreement through friendship or at least a respectful acquaintance like teachers or preachers in order for another person to call her by name.

Molly just shrugged her shoulders and headed for the door. She and Noah hopped on their bikes, leaving Officer Wolfe standing at the door still waiting for an answer.

Nobody noticed Tom Flaky's head poking

through the swinging door, listening to every word.

CHAPTER
6

Randy Pepper peered out the kitchen window, noting the blue car around the corner still parked under the tree. It wasn't the same car as last week, but he could tell even from this distance that the driver inside hadn't changed.

After a quick shower and a bite to eat, he picked up his phone and dialed. He could hear the music in the background before the familiar voice started to speak. First, Randy Pepper relayed the most current, relevant information, and then he asked about Molly. The voice reassured Randy that tonight everything was going to go just as planned.

Randy asked for the details one more time, and then proceeded to the front porch where he waited for Molly to return. He didn't know if he could go through with this, knowing the truth might be too big a thing for Molly right now.

But, he also knew it wasn't right keeping it from her, either. And, he'd promised Molly's mother that he'd mend her broken promise.

CHAPTER

7

That Dark, Jumpy Feeling

Before turning the corner onto their street, Molly skidded to a stop. Noah swerved, narrowly avoiding Molly on the left and a parked car on the right.

"Hey! What did you stop for?" he yelled, panting.

But Molly was unfazed. She was contemplating the sight of an old-fashioned blue car parked under an oak tree around the corner from her house. With chrome trim and white hubcaps, it looked like something out of an old TV show—except here in the two thousands, it seemed especially out of place.

Molly had never seen it before in her neighborhood, and considered herself an expert at knowing who was who and what their business was around here.

Noah started to protest again, but Molly held out her hand for silence at the first sign of movement in the front seat of the car, as if someone had ducked out of sight in an attempt to hide.

"Did you see that?" she whispered.

"See what?"

"There, in the car," she pointed.

But there was nothing to see. Not anymore. The front seat of the car now appeared empty. Noah still held a grudge against Molly for almost killing him, and started up again, riding out in front of her, right past the car without saying a word, as if proving to Molly she was seeing things.

But that dark, jumpy feeling that slowly creeps up on you somehow clung to Molly's mind, and now she felt uneasy, like maybe somebody was watching her.

Or following her. Or *worse*...

Hoping to chase that creepy feeling away, Molly followed Noah's lead, and zoomed right past the old car. But as soon as she approached her driveway, the blue car suddenly rumbled to life and pulled away from the curb.

Molly stopped and turned around as it drove

off, wondering if Noah saw it, too.

She couldn't wonder for very long, however, because her dad was waiting for her on the front porch with arms crossed, a dead-serious look on his face.

"Where were you?" he called, almost scaring Molly right off her bike.

"We went into town to get a doughnut," she answered casually, walking her bicycle up the driveway and leaning it against the front steps.

"Why didn't you leave me a note?"

"I forgot," Molly said, though she instantly regretted using the "f" word because that only made her father go into lecture mode. Being a policeman can make you overprotective, even paranoid. Forgetting to leave a note in the Pepper household was a major offense.

Molly searched for backup from Noah, but it appeared he had already seen Officer Pepper waiting for them on the front porch, and had left Molly to face him alone.

Molly remained quiet while her dad lectured her about things she already knew. She noticed he looked especially tired and ragged today. Sometimes she felt bad for him, for having to be serious and in charge all the time, instead of like before...back when he would take Molly and her mother to Giants' games and museums, or just play soccer with her in the backyard.

On days like today, when Molly could see that heaviness building up behind his eyes, she tried not to take it too personally. But it was hard when he looked at her like that—like nothing in the world could make him happy.

When he finished his lecture, Molly tried to point out that she'd never anticipated being gone long enough for him to notice, but that just made him lecture even more because nobody who ends up dead or missing ever *thinks* they will be gone long enough for someone to notice.

Molly could see his point, but still didn't believe it deserved this kind of response. In order to avoid punishment, she quietly withstood his lecture, and then brushed past him into the house, stopping at the last second to apologize. "Dad—"

But, he cut her off before she could get any part of an apology out. "You need some time to think about being more responsible," he said, almost sorrowfully.

That did not sound good. "What does that mean?" she asked, certain she already knew what he meant, but decided on further clarification.

He folded his arms and frowned even harder. "You're grounded for the rest of the day."

"What? Dad!"

The only thing Molly lamented about her punishment was the impact it would have on her possible plans to hike up Candlestick Hill tonight. Her school was small; most of her friends had left for camps or vacations and summer homes. So, it wasn't a party she might miss out on or a sleepover that would go on without her.

Summer for Molly Pepper usually involved more simple things—collecting shells on the beach, people-watching at the dock, riding in the back of her dad's police car; nothing too exciting. To her, summer meant freedom.

Even though she hadn't decided one way or another about climbing Candlestick Hill—the idea that she got to choose whether or not to go was part of the thrill. *The adventure.*

Not anymore.

Molly felt her cheeks burning, and that simmering feeling brought on earlier by Officer Wolfe's out-of-line questions bloomed inside her once again, stronger than ever.

That's when Molly couldn't help herself. She lifted her head to find her dad's familiar eyes, and said the one thing she knew would hurt him the most. Because at that moment, Molly wanted him to hurt more than her.

"I wish mom was here instead of you," she

said, hoping she didn't mean it. But, the thing was—Molly didn't know if that was true. And the thought of not knowing was what scared her the most.

Randy Pepper didn't blink. Molly wanted him to blink; she willed those lids to shut so she wouldn't have to look anymore at the pain behind his eyes. But he remained frozen there in front of her, and now Molly hurt even more.

She hung her head low and trudged into the house, straight to her room. At the corner of her bed, her foot collided with a shoebox she'd left on the floor a few days ago when she was especially missing her mother. Molly hesitated picking it up, knowing already what was inside, and not sure if she wanted to revisit the past. But after a few seconds, she couldn't help herself, and knelt down to lift the lid.

Inside were the things her mother wanted Molly to have—her old jewelry and washed-out photos of curly, blond-haired Molly covered in a sprinkling of freckles. She was smiling inside her mother's embrace, oblivious to the facts of life, completely unaware that her mother would leave her.

Molly returned the photos to the box and picked up a dulled, gold band speckled with three tiny diamonds...Mom's wedding ring. She had told Molly to take care of it until she returned. But, Molly didn't want her mother's old things. She wanted *her*.

She slammed the lid shut and shoved the box behind a row of dusty stuffed animals in the back of the closet.

Then, she threw herself on her bed to have another look at her mysterious letter.

**IF ADVENTURE
IS YOUR DESIRE
GO TO
174 CANDLESTICK HILL
AT NINE O'CLOCK TONIGHT
NO SOONER
NO LATER**

It was decided.

Molly would figure a way out of this place, away from all of this disappointment and up that hill—despite being grounded, despite Candlestick Hill being the steepest hill in the country.

And she would get Noah to go with her, because she couldn't bear it alone.

CHAPTER
8

Ruby Dodd was just finishing the last of a corned beef sandwich when a cop car rounded the corner and stopped right behind her. She watched in her rearview mirror as the driver's side door opened, spilling a tall figure into the street.

He left the car running and slammed the door shut, looking over his shoulder the entire time. The faint crunching sound of his black lace-up shoes drew closer and closer until he stood beside Ruby's door and leaned into the open window, his arms resting above him on the car's roof.

"She wouldn't talk," said the cop to Ruby.

"Just what I thought. I don't think she knows anything."

"What about you?"

"Nothing much is turning up here, either," Ruby said, turning her head away from her visitor for a minute. She removed her wire-rimmed glasses and wiped them on her sleeve before returning them to the tip of her nose. "But, I'm still convinced tonight is the night."

"How can you be so sure?"

"Because it's the 13th! And, I'm almost positive that the UPS delivery this morning was a message from him. Who else would hand deliver a letter and nothing else?"

"I don't know—"

"We will follow her all day and night until he turns up, do you understand? I am *not* letting him get away this time."

"I gotta get back to the station, Ruby," said the cop, stepping away from the car. "I still have procedure to follow, you know."

"This *better* be it," Ruby said, throwing her fist in the air. "I haven't waited five years for nothing."

The cop ran his hands through his thick, dark hair, and returned to his car. As he drove away, he wondered if the infamous agent Dodd was a little more *nut-so* than he'd originally thought. He figured he'd find out one way or another before the night was over.

CHAPTER 9

The Hill With Ski Run Potential

At seven o'clock, Officer Pepper left for work, leaving Sarah, Noah's older sister, in charge. Molly's dad always insisted on a babysitter the nights he worked the graveyard shift, reasoning Molly was only twelve and not particularly responsible yet (though Molly disagreed).

Sarah's job was to make sure Molly made it to bed on time and didn't get kidnapped by bad guys. So far she had an excellent track record. She usually came around eight o'clock, but tonight with Molly being grounded, Officer Pepper asked her to arrive an hour early, just in case.

"In case *what?*" Molly asked, after Sarah had

made herself comfortable in front of the TV.

Randy placed his hands on his daughter's shoulders and squatted down until their eyes were level. He seemed more distant than usual, though Molly knew it was because of the horrible thing she'd said to him. Still, she couldn't figure out how to take it back or say sorry, other than giving him her best hug before he left.

When they were eye to eye, Molly felt like she was looking into a dark, cloudy sky. "Be safe tonight, Molls, okay?"

"I'm stuck at home, Dad. How dangerous of a place do you think this is?"

"I just—" he looked away and drew in a deep breath. "Just remember how much I love you," he said, finding her eyes again, the eyes of her mother.

Molly didn't know how to respond, and threw her arms around his neck, wondering why this moment felt so big. Her dad was just going to work, right? Just like any other night.

At eight thirty, Molly only had to get past Sarah, who had proven easy to evade in episodes past, as she was always either glued to her phone or the TV. It was Noah's parents Molly was worried about, for whom they formulated a plan: Noah would claim to go to bed early, and then sneak out at eight-thirty.

For Molly, sneaking out was a piece of cake since her window screen was already out and shoved behind her bed from her last escape (if there ever was a bright side to your dad working all night, sneaking out was it).

Noah, on the other hand, needed a little more help being rebellious, so it was a good thing he had Molly for a friend. However, his window was on the second floor, so Molly suggested he wait until he knew his parents would be glued to the TV, and then quietly sneak down the back stairs and out the back door.

It seemed an easy task, considering Noah's parents watched their TV shows on schedule every night. But, Molly still worried.

Noah miraculously succeeded without incident, because at eight-thirty on the dot he showed up at the lamppost between their houses dressed head-to-toe in black. The sun wasn't quite down yet, though, so he looked a little suspicious.

Molly had kept her outfit stylish yet practical—a dark purple velour hoodie and matching sweatpants. That way, she could pass for a normal kid out on a bike ride, and wouldn't look like she was ready to rob a bank.

"I don't know about this," Noah mused, as they walked their bikes to the corner of the street. "What if my parents decide to check in on me tonight?"

"Do they normally check in on you? You're almost thirteen, you know."

"How would I know if they checked in on me? I'm usually asleep by the time they go to bed."

"Well, then, I guess you'll find out tonight, won't you?"

"That's doesn't sound very promising."

"Then quit thinking about it. This might be a once-in-a-lifetime adventure. You think you'd be willing to take a few risks," Molly chided as they hopped on their bikes and pedaled across the street.

"I'm just worried about what's going to happen to me if they find out I snuck out of the house."

"So what? You get grounded for a day. Big deal. You have to learn to put things into perspective when you're breaking rules."

Noah was quiet after that.

Molly wasn't really sure why Noah always insisted on being so obedient all the time. The way she saw it, Noah needed to mess up occasionally. That way, people wouldn't always expect perfection out of him. And, if anybody, Noah's parents expected perfection.

It only took a minute for them to bike to the bottom of Candlestick Hill. Noah arrived first and waited for Molly.

She pulled up beside him. "Don't tell me that this isn't the most exciting thing you've ever done," she said, feeling a grin just above her chin. It felt like a nice replacement to the frown she'd had earlier while getting grounded.

Adventure had a way of cheering anybody up.

After propping their bikes up against a wooden fence, they started climbing the hill. Noah was silent, probably due to the fact that he was out of breath. He wasn't one for exercise, despite his claim with goal number two. The sun had just dipped behind the horizon. Neither spoke; both were too busy breathing. Molly stared at her feet, hoping for the narrow, focused perspective to make the climb easier to endure.

It didn't.

Occasionally she'd look up, noting the colorful two and three-story houses popping up from the ground, almost perpendicular to the hill. They looked playful compared to the rigid incline on which she and Noah had found themselves.

About halfway up, they heard the increasing sound of a car climbing the hill behind them.

Molly slipped behind a mailbox for cover. Noah stood in the middle of the sidewalk, watching her quizzically, until Molly motioned for him to join her.

"Why are we hiding?" he whispered from behind a pink bougainvillea bush.

"We don't want anybody to see us," said Molly as the car slowly passed.

"Other than our parents, do you really think anybody cares?"

But, Molly wasn't listening. She had her eye on the tail end of the old-fashioned blue car. It was nearly up the hill now, and looked very similar to the one parked on the street by her house.

"Noah!" Molly said, once the car had crested the hill. "Did you see that?"

Noah stepped out from his hiding spot to join Molly as they continued their treacherous climb. "Yes," he said between huffs and puffs. "It was a car. Those things do drive up streets."

Molly wacked Noah on the arm. "I'm serious. It was the same one as before, the one parked down on our street."

"How can you tell? All I saw were the taillights."

"I'm positive."

But, Noah wasn't convinced. They continued

debating whether or not the blue car was indeed the same one as before, not even realizing they had reached the top of the hill until they were standing at the end of the dead-end street. However, Molly and Noah were so out of breath from arguing and climbing, they couldn't even congratulate each other on their accomplishment.

The blue car in question was parked on the far side of the street between two driveways. Molly immediately crept over to inspect it, but found the interior empty and the light of the moon too faint now to determine its true shade of blue.

Not only that, but while Molly inspected the blue car, Noah stood in the circle of lamplight shining down on the rusty, old mailbox marked 174. But, when he looked behind the mailbox for a house, all he could find was an empty hill.

There was no 174 Candlestick Hill.

CHAPTER 10

One Lucky Amigo

"Where's the *house?*" Noah asked, throwing his hands up in the air. "Are you sure it's number 174?"

Molly rushed over to see for herself, and then checked the note. "Yes. That's what it says: 174 Candlestick Hill."

"Maybe it's a typo."

"No, no. It *has* to be here." Molly turned in a circle, making eye contact with every single house at the top of Candlestick Hill.

"I don't know about this," said Noah, stepping out of the light and into the grassy field behind the mailbox.

"But there *aren't* any more houses," Molly said, feeling the weight of disappointment settling on top of her. *No...this can't be right.*

The long blades of grass swooshed against Noah's pants as he hiked back to the mailbox where Molly had slouched against the post. He could see in her eyes the look of disappointment; it was a look he knew too well.

"I guess it really was just a dumb practical joke," Molly muttered, trying not to let the sting of disappointment make her bitter. But, she couldn't help it. She kicked the post with her foot, and sunk to the ground with her head in her hands.

But, Noah wasn't giving up. He hadn't sneaked out of bed and risked groundation only to be shut down like this, nor did he want Molly's night to be ruined. He scoured the shadows all around the mailbox, as if expecting a house to be hiding somewhere behind the skinny post. "What did the note say, again? Maybe we missed something."

Molly read through the entire message once more. "If adventure is your desire go to 174 Candlestick Hill at 9:00 tonight. No sooner. No later. That's what it says," Molly said, passing the note off to Noah, and knocking her head back into the post.

Noah stared at it hard, and then slowly rotated in a circle, finally stopping where he'd started—directly in front of the black, rusty mailbox marked with the number 174 in faded yellow paint.

174.

Noah's gaze dropped to Molly, his eyes wide. "The mailbox!" he yelled.

She jumped up, and together they opened the lid. Noah shined his flashlight. Inside, a small, black box waited in the dark, cramped space, all by itself.

Molly pulled it out.

"What is it?" asked Noah.

"I don't know," she said, brushing her finger across the gold number 13 printed on top.

She tipped the lid open at its hinges. A small, brass key lay at the bottom of the gold-lined box. Molly picked it up, and noticed an engraving of some kind carved into the metal. Noah leaned in closer until his flashlight beam was centered directly on the engraving, and they could make out three distinct words: **THE NIGHT TRAIN.**

"The Night Train?" Noah said out loud, laughing as if it were all a big joke.

Molly didn't know what to say. Or think. Because she had already concluded that the Night Train was a rumor, just a figment of someone's imagination (certainly not hers). Yet, here she was, holding two objects in her hand that clearly said otherwise.

"Do you think it's all one big joke?" Molly asked, even as she wondered how a joke could be this realistic.

"I don't think so," said Noah, taking the box for further inspection.

But Molly still wasn't ready to believe in the unbelievable.

Yet, how could she refute solid evidence sitting right there in the palm of her hand?

Maybe, just maybe, the Night Train. *Was.* Real.

She finally let loose a grin, even though what she really wanted to do was jump up and down and scream at the top of her lungs because she couldn't remember the last time anything even remotely exciting or magical had happened to her, especially since her mother left.

In fact, Molly had specifically dropped *exciting* and *magical* from her vocabulary on that very day.

Now, as she stood at the top of Candlestick Hill staring down at a key clearly marked with evidence that the Night Train was real, Molly didn't know if she dared to believe in something again.

"Do you realize what this means?" Noah asked, still studying the box.

"I think so," replied Molly, thinking but not really knowing for sure she really *did* know what it meant, other than the fact that her life had just gotten a lot more exciting. And her pessimism had been knocked down a peg.

Noah aimed the flashlight down into the square box as if he were looking for something else. "Either you've been holding out on me about how much money you have, or you're one lucky amigo."

Molly finally looked up. "Do you really think I have a hundred bucks just hanging around, ready to spend on a lottery?"

"Exactly. Which means…" Noah stuck out his hand like they were meeting for the first time. Molly wasn't sure what he was doing, but played along and graciously shook his hand. "You are officially the luckiest person I know. Nice to meet you."

Molly felt goofy shaking Noah's hand, and released it as soon as she could.

"But, that doesn't make any sense," she protested. "I didn't enter the lottery! I don't even have a hundred dollars. Not even close."

Noah tipped the box upside down and shook it back and forth. "I guess that means somebody wants you to have a ride on the Night Train, then."

"They do?" Molly asked, feeling confused by the whole thing now. "Who would want that?"

"Beats me. But I wouldn't complain too much about it if I were you."

"I'm not complaining. I'm just confused," Molly said, wondering what Noah was looking for. He seemed to be digging into the empty box like it was hiding buried treasure.

Suddenly, the box slipped out of Noah's hands and dropped to the ground, leaving something gold stuck in between his fingers.

"A-ha!" he said, holding a small square piece of gold paper up to the light.

CHAPTER

11

Doors, Gates and What Awaits

"What is that?" Molly asked, staring at the square of gold paper in Noah's hand.

"It was stuck in the bottom of the box."

"It was?"

"Yes."

"*What* is it?"

"Here, hold the flashlight."

Molly did as Noah asked and shined the light on another message printed in the same font as Molly's mysterious letter. It appeared to be some sort of riddle.

Adventure awaits
Through a door marked with 8
Twenty paces from the post

Turn right at the gate
Tho' burned to the ground
You will find the stairs sound
At the door, don't knock once
But twice to get down

"A riddle!" Molly exclaimed, shifting up on her toes. "We get to solve a riddle!"

"Actually, it's really more like a set of directions."

Molly rolled her eyes. "Seriously? Like the specifics of it matter?"

Noah ignored her. Molly returned the box to the mailbox for safekeeping, and then tucked the key into her pocket and read through the riddle one more time.

Noah stood by the mailbox post. "I'm guessing the directions are talking about *this* post, don't you think?"

"It's the only post *I* can see."

Noah placed his right foot at the base of the mailbox post. Molly joined him, planting her foot right beside his.

"Okay then." Noah took a step and started counting, but Molly pulled him back.

"Hold on," she said. "Do you suppose it means big steps or small steps?"

Noah contemplated for a moment. "It

probably doesn't matter. Let's just start walking."

"Okay. On the count of three." Molly held onto Noah's wrist. "One. Two. Three."

Together they stepped away from the post, each stride through the long grass taking them further into the darkness and away from the fuzzy glow of lamplight.

They advanced while counting each step out loud, their voices echoing at the top of Candlestick Hill on a breezy, starry night. Finally, at the count of twenty, they stopped just past a pile of broken boards protruding from the ground.

"What do the instructions say next?" asked Noah.

Molly referred to the riddle card in her hand. "Turn right at the gate."

Noah aimed the flashlight out in front of them. They scanned the empty lot and the charred, broken boards at their feet, where an old, deteriorating square of wood hung from a pair of rusty metal hinges. A creaking noise eked from the hinges as the board swished back and forth in the breeze.

"It's not much of a gate anymore, is it?" said Molly, looking down.

"Good enough for me." Noah pivoted right and treaded through the grass again. He hesitated at each movement, his steps long and pronounced.

"Hey, wait up," Molly started up after him, but stopped at the sound of something hollow beneath her feet. She stomped down hard on what felt and sounded like wood. "Noah!"

He turned.

"Down here," she said, stomping on the board.

Noah lowered the light, illuminating Molly's shoes. "What is it?" he asked.

Molly fell to her knees and brushed the palms of her hands along the flat, rough surface. "I think it's a trapdoor!" she said, feeling a bubble of excitement fizzing up inside her.

Noah set the flashlight down and knelt beside Molly. They each took one side of the hollow, wooden square and followed the outline of a groove all the way around until their fingers met up at the bottom, directly under a spot where the number 8 was crudely carved into the wood.

"It's the number 8, Noah!"

"I see it!"

Noah rotated the light, revealing a small keyhole underneath the number 8. Molly retrieved the key from her pocket and pushed it straight into the keyhole.

It fit perfectly.

With a hard turn, she rotated it clockwise until it caught at the sound of a metallic click.

"This is it," she said, pulling out the key and sliding her fingers into the bottom groove of the trapdoor.

The hinges screeched as she pulled upward, releasing the cool, heavy odor of must and dirt. Noah shined the light on a set of uneven wooden stairs leading downward.

Molly consulted her riddle card again. "I think we're supposed to go down the stairs," she said with a smile so big that her cheeks hurt.

But, when she looked up at Noah, he wasn't smiling at all. In fact, he looked like he was about to hyperventilate.

"Noah, what's wrong?"

"I'm not going under the ground again," Noah replied firmly, backing away from the door.

CHAPTER 12

Between six and eight o'clock, Main Street started to wind down, though in the summer the restaurants and ice cream stands usually remained open until ten. Soon, more than half of Blue Rock Island's employees would make their way back down to the dock to catch the commute ferry back to San Francisco or the east bay.

Flaky's Fantastic Doughnuts was one of the few shops to remain open until eleven, just in case somebody had a craving for a doughnut at an odd hour.

Somebody always did.

So, when Officer Pepper drove past the doughnut shop at eight o'clock, just as he was instructed to do, he was surprised to find the lights out and the *closed* sign hung clearly in the front window.

He pulled to a stop in one of the diagonal parking spaces facing the dark store, and slowly walked up to the front door. First, he tried the door handle to verify that indeed it was locked, rather than something fishy going on like a burglary. But, when the handle didn't move, Officer Pepper placed his hands against the glass and peered into the store, noting everything seemed to be in perfect order.

Strange, he thought to himself. He had talked to Tom Flaky, earlier that day, who made no mention of closing the shop early.

Officer Pepper returned to his car, wondering if he should call it into the station— just in case. But, he decided against it when he opened the car door and found a grocery sack sitting on the seat.

After rifling through it, he wasn't quite sure he was ready for this next part of the plan. Or, if he was too thrilled about it, either. But, at this point, he supposed it didn't really matter what he had to do, as long as he made things right.

He slipped back into the front seat of his car, wondering if by now Molly had sneaked out of the house like he expected she would. He knew her well enough to realize that grounding her had been the only thing to ensure she climb up that hill.

CHAPTER 13

Tunnel Vision

A salty breeze had picked up, making Molly wonder if she would wake to more fog in the morning. The thought made her pause and look out across the bay for any sign of incoming gloom, but so far the night was clear, and every direction she looked speckled with little white lights.

With his arms folded in front of him, Noah sulked a few feet away from Molly. She swished through the grass and tapped him on the shoulder, and tried to speak cheerfully. "Noah, relax. It's totally different than the crawl space under your house. You can't even compare the two."

"How do you know?"

"Because this *leads* somewhere. *I think,*" Molly said, though it didn't seem to help at all. "I know it *looks* the same...with the trapdoor and all... but, this is the way to the Night Train! It's supposed to be fun and exciting!"

Noah finally turned around, scowling. "Just looking down there makes me wish I was back at home, in bed."

"How about I go down first?" Molly suggested, trying to be brave. She didn't *want* to go down there all by herself, but it was starting to look like she didn't have a choice.

"I don't know...."

Somehow the idea of being brave made Molly *feel* brave, like she was an adult trying to reassure a little kid there were no monsters under his bed. Or, in this case, trying to reassure her best friend that if *she* could descend a staircase leading under the earth in the dark, that he could, too. Especially if they did it together.

"I'll just check it out. You don't have to go if you really don't want to, but I'll bet it's not as bad as you think."

Noah seemed to consider that, and Molly waited for an answer, hoping he wouldn't decide to wimp out on her, after coming so far. Not only because she would prefer not to have to go down the steps alone, but also because she knew Noah was tougher than this. And she knew he could do it.

"Okay," he finally agreed. "But make it fast. I don't really like the idea of you being down there and me being up here all by ourselves."

Molly grabbed the flashlight and swung her legs over the edge of the trapdoor until they were barely skimming the top of the first stair. "See? The stairs are solid. That's a good sign." Her feet shuffled forward, carefully sliding along and then dropping down to the next step.

She was under total control...*total control.*

Once Molly's head had cleared the trapdoor, she shined the flashlight in front of her to inspect her surroundings. It seemed she was enclosed on all sides by brick and stone.

She continued down, counting eleven stairs in all, and then turned left, and stopped, and then right, and stopped...wondering why it seemed like the stairs led straight down into a brick cellar the size of a dumpster.

The breath inside her was shrinking, becoming more and more shallow by the second... and her clothes suddenly felt too tight, the thick air heavy and suffocating.

Where were her cinnamon bears when she needed them?

She spun around, ready to dash back up the stairs and free herself, when her flashlight skimmed a spot where the wall met the ceiling. She rotated the light back to the top corner of the wall, stopping on a small sign that had an arrow pointing to the left.

On the sign, beside the arrow was one word: **TRAIN.**

Molly drew in a sharp breath.

"You okay?" Noah called, his voice echoing down the stairs.

Molly spun around, aiming the light up at Noah's feet. "Noah! You *have* to come down here!" she yelled, the sound of her voice ricocheting off every surface like a Ping-Pong ball gone awry. "It's nothing like what you're imagining. I promise."

But Noah wasn't moving.

"Here," said Molly, tossing him the flashlight. It landed with a thud at the top of the steps. A space of silence followed while she waited for him to either pick it up or walk away, or at least to say something. But it seemed as if Noah had turned into a statue.

"Noah?"

Finally, movement.

Noah grabbed the flashlight and shined it in Molly's eyes, then hesitantly took his first step.

And another…and another, until he had finally reached the bottom and was standing beside her.

"You're right. This isn't so bad," he said warily, as if trying to convince himself. "At least I can stand up straight."

But, there was no time for celebrating. As soon as he was beside her, Molly reclaimed the flashlight and aimed it straight up at the sign. "Look!" she said.

"Where does it point to?" Noah asked. "I thought this was a dead-end."

"That's what I thought, too. But, *watch*," she said, moving sideways. In an instant, her body had partially disappeared behind the wall.

"Hey, how'd you do that?"

"It's a hallway," Molly said. "A hidden one. Come *on*."

Noah held his breath and followed Molly, surprised as each step found them further along. Molly led the way as they ambled through the narrow opening for another twenty feet until the space around them widened.

She shined the light down the dark corridor. It seemed to end fifteen or so feet away at an arched, wooden door made of thick, wide planks.

"Look!" Molly said, tugging at Noah's sleeve, catching the door's outline with her light.

They raced to the end of the hall, stopping at

the planked door. The top of the doorway formed an arch, and the number 13 was carved into the wood at the highest point of the curve.

Molly drew the beam of light from the number 13 downward to an old, brass doorknob. But, when she tried turning the knob, it didn't move.

"What do we do now?" she asked. "Knock?"

"Maybe…" Noah said, wiggling the doorknob, too, as if it would somehow only open for him. "Wait. That's it!" he said.

"What?"

"*Knock.* Remember the instruction card?"

"You mean, the riddle card?"

"Fine. *Riddle.* It said something about knocking. Where's the card?"

Molly held it up under the light.

"*Don't knock once but twice.* There you have it," Noah said, flicking the card with his finger.

Molly knocked, just like she was supposed to. She then tilted her head sideways and listened for…Molly wasn't sure, really… But the card said to knock twice. So she knocked.

Twice.

The door didn't immediately offer anything in response, which worried Molly a little bit. But, she didn't know what else to do now that they had done everything the riddle had asked. She figured it was somebody else's turn now.

So, she waited.

Noah waited, too, tapping his foot on the dusty stone floor.

Molly pressed her ear against the rough surface of the boards, and Noah found a spot beside her, his ear pressed up next to hers until their faces were only inches apart...listening...

The knob started to turn.

Molly's heart did a double dribble. Noah realized he was sweating.

They stepped backward just as the door swung open towards them.

CHAPTER

14

Officer Wolfe stared down into the dark depths of the trapdoor opening. There was no way he planned on following those two kids down there, no matter what Ruby told him to do. Why did she get the easy job, anyway–just hanging out at the station, waiting for his report? Probably eating doughnuts and sipping hot chocolate right now.

Officer Wolfe's stomach growled.

He wasn't sure why he'd signed up for this case. Following a twelve-year-old kid and her father was not his idea of the kind of intrigue he'd expected. Still, he reasoned he had to climb the career ladder rung by rung to get to the top, and this was just one of those rungs.

After parking Ruby's car at the top of the hill,

he'd hidden himself behind two fat pine trees tucked away in the shadows. Unfortunately, he'd planted himself a little too far from the mailbox to hear the exact conversation between the two kids. However, once they seemed after something, he followed their steps to this very spot, though this was as far as he planned on going.

Now, he'd report his findings: that Molly Pepper and her companion were following a set of clues that had led them down into a tunnel.

Officer Wolfe knew where the tunnel would take them. Just after his arrival on the island last month, he'd studied the map of Blue Rock Island like he was taking a final exam. The island was riddled with interconnecting tunnels, all leading to an old, defunct train station that apparently was home to the Night Train.

And, it looked like the Pepper girl had been invited to climb aboard.

CHAPTER

15

A Sinking Feeling

Just inside the dimly lit doorway stood a tall man whose face seemed to pull downward along with his nose. He looked much older than Molly's dad, especially without any hair covering his shiny round head.

His appearance made Molly nervous, depleting her of any courage to at least smile or say hello. Her mind started to race. Could this man be a kidnapper or worse?

Molly moved in closer to Noah and scrutinized the tall man's face. There was something about him, something about his crescent-shaped eyes and official-looking uniform all trimmed in black and gold that made her take a deep breath and count to five.

She finally smiled.

He smiled, too. "Welcome," he said, his voice heavy with an English accent.

"I…we…" Molly glanced at Noah, and then she just stopped talking altogether because her mind had gone blank. What did she even want to say?

The Englishman saved her from any further worry by propping the door open with a gloved hand. "Right this way, Miss Pepper."

Molly was taken aback at the sound of her name. How did he know who she was?

Noah stepped through the arched doorway first, but Molly followed right behind. Once they were inside, the door squeaked shut and the man gave the knob a quick turn. It clicked, leaving them standing in total darkness.

Molly thought about screaming.

A flickering of lights around the rim of the ceiling illuminated what appeared to be a circular, stone room containing only one door—the door they had just come through. Molly instantly understood that there was nowhere to go but right back out the door that had just been locked behind them.

A chill scurried along the back of her neck, and she wondered what she was doing here in this small, cramped room with this strange man. The look of fear on Noah's face let her know that he was questioning this whole thing, too.

"Please hold on," said the Englishman calmly, as if being stuck in a stone closet with two kids was the most normal thing in the world.

Hold on? *To what?*

Molly held her breath. That's what she held.

The Englishman pressed some kind of button hidden somewhere along the wall between the stones and bricks. The entryway began to lower just like the Haunted House ride at Disneyland. Except, here there were no stretching paintings. And this wasn't a *ride*. And Molly still didn't know whether or not she would see blue sky again.

When the sinking entryway came to a stop, the Englishman brought his hand over the doorknob, and turned it.

Molly exhaled, wondering what was on the other side of the door.

"Follow me, please," he said.

Noah had since turned a very pale shade of green, making Molly wonder if he might pass out. She kept an eye on him, just in case.

They stepped out into a dimly lit brick tunnel that seemed to extend forever in both directions. The air felt cool and wet, and was filled with the same musty scent as the crawl space under Noah's house and the passageway from which they'd come.

The sound of slowly dripping water echoed throughout the tunnel, making Molly feel cold. Other than that, the only other sounds came from the Englishman and his two young companions; it appeared as if they were the only visitors here.

Molly looked above her to find pendant light fixtures suspended from the ceiling, casting their golden hue along the brick walls. She peered over the edge of the walkway, where old, wooden and steel train tracks covered the ground five feet below.

Train tracks!

Molly brought her attention back to the Englishman, wondering what she was supposed to do next. She figured there was more to the Night Train riddle than this, but didn't really know how to go about finding it, now that she'd completed her set of directions on her golden card. And, she certainly wasn't going to jump down there.

Without saying a word, the Englishman pointed to the ground. Molly and Noah directed their eyes to a small, square plaque by their feet. It blended almost too well into the brick pattern on the floor. Just like the previous sign, this one, too, had a left-pointing arrow beside a single word: **TRAIN.**

"I guess we go that way," Noah said, taking a few steps to the left.

Molly followed him, but turned for one more look at the Englishman. He had already disappeared.

CHAPTER
16

The Light at the End of the Tunnel

"Where is everyone else?" Molly asked as they passed under another yellow light. She much preferred the darker stretches of shadows to these ugly spurts of yellow glaring in her eyes.

"I don't know." Noah's voice was quiet and hesitant as their feet tip-tapped along the brick walkway.

Just as the tunnel started to curve inward, they heard a low rumbling of what sounded like an engine. A *big* one.

Molly's heart thumped louder as they ran toward the sound, toward a haze of lights and voices growing brighter and louder the closer they got.

When they came out of the curve, Molly

stopped first, breathing hard. There, in front of her was the Night Train. Light spread up from the train tracks and out across the tunnel as a haze of smoke encircled them.

"Whoa," said Noah.

Headlights blared from the train's nose as smoke puffed up from the ground. It was a shiny, sleek black, with an occasional touch of gold or red in the details. Centered inside a black rectangle on the train's nose was the number 1331, painted in gold.

Molly stepped closer. "This is the real deal." She pressed her hand against the nose of the train, loving how the paint felt slick as glass on her skin.

"Six minutes until departure," came an announcement through a loudspeaker.

Molly watched a grinning teenage boy and his mother who seemed just as mesmerized skip up a short set of stairs into the third train car. It made her wonder how they had gotten their invitation—if they'd forked out a hundred bucks, or had been mysteriously invited, like her.

"We better keep moving," said Noah, pointing at a woman who had snuck up behind them.

Molly turned around.

"Hello there." The woman smiled. She was

much shorter and stockier than the tall Englishman, but wore an identical uniform and a little black cap to hide her curly white hair. In her hands she held a digital tablet, which she handed to Molly. "Type your name," the train official instructed, pointing to the screen.

Molly obeyed. When she finished, the screen lit up in red and gold with the words: *Welcome to the Night Train, Molly Pepper.*

The train official took the tablet back and held out her hand. "Now, as soon as you give me your key, Miss Pepper, you may have your train ticket."

"My key?" Molly repeated, feeling a little sad about having to relinquish her newest prize already. It would have made a nice souvenir. Still, she obeyed and dropped the key into the train official's hand. She tucked it somewhere inside her blazer jacket, and rustled around in there for a second, like she was searching for something.

Molly held her breath, waiting.

Noah tapped his foot.

All at once, the train official withdrew her hand from her jacket and held up a shiny black card with words printed in gold along the front:

• Molly Pepper •
Admission for two
The Night Train
June 13th
Car 2 • Row 8

"Noah!" Molly exclaimed. "It says *'Admission for two!'*"

He swiped the ticket away from her. "Let me see that."

Sure enough, it looked like Molly wouldn't be boarding the Night Train alone. Not only did she have a golden ticket with her very own name printed on the front, but she would get to share it with her very best friend.

Noah wanted to hug her, but he erred on the side of caution and gave her a high five instead. But his half-moon grin said everything.

CHAPTER 17

Officer Wolfe showed their tickets to the attendant standing at the top of the stairs, wishing the old man would just hurry up. Ruby had already elbowed him twice, reminding him to smile, and pretending to be as enamored with the train as the rest of the passengers in order to avoid suspicion.

It hadn't been difficult for two FBI agents to snag a pair of tickets for the train. All they had to do was find one of the many tunnel entrances, then show their badges and demand a seat. Wolfe almost felt sorry for the poor saps whose places they'd taken.

Oh well. Life wasn't fair—that much he'd learned, and it was better to figure it out sooner rather than later.

They found their seats in the very back of car number one. The long, red velvet benches proved very roomy, something Officer Wolfe was grateful for with his long, lanky legs. Ruby wouldn't know the first thing about needing extra legroom, he thought, as he stared at her pudgy legs that seemed to barely touch the wooden floor beneath them.

"You keep an eye out for the girl," Ruby whispered as she pulled her phone out of her purse. "I'll look for Moody."

Wolfe rolled his eyes. "How many times have you *told* me? I know my job."

"Well, you'd better hope this little train escapade leads us to him, or you won't have a job in the morning."

"Relax, Ruby. I told you, she'll be here."

"How can you be sure? What if she chickens out at the last second?"

"*Everybody* comes, Ruby. Now quit bugging me so I can concentrate." Officer Wolfe wished for once Ruby would stop second-guessing everything.

But, maybe that's what chasing after a ghost for five years does—makes you paranoid.

Hopefully he'd never find out for himself.

Wolfe turned his head away from Ruby just

as a blonde, curly-haired girl came into view down on the platform. He nudged Ruby, and she took a deep breath, trying to hide her sense of relief.

Wolfe wanted to say, 'I told you so,' but remained quiet.

CHAPTER

18

A Car With a View

A total of four cars were attached to the engine, which Molly didn't think was very big for a train. But, who was she to complain?

They stopped at car number two, and Molly and Noah bounded up the steps. An old man with golden-dark skin, almond eyes and a dimple on his chin stood at the top of the stairs collecting tickets. He smiled as Molly showed him her ticket.

"Welcome to the Night Train, Molly Pepper," he said.

Molly grinned at her personalized greeting.

When they stepped inside, Molly forgot about everything else as she gaped at the glass roof above her. She'd never seen a glass roof for anything, let alone one on top of a train! The window started at eye level on either side of the train, and then swooped upward into a dome. She could even see the rafters all the way up in the roof.

"Wow," she said, taking in the rest of the car.

Fuzzy, dark red benches hugged both sides of the train, each bench positioned underneath a window, and a wide aisle in between. The air smelled clean and newly polished, including the smooth wooden floor beneath their feet.

"What row are we?" asked Noah.

"Eight," said Molly as she cruised down the aisle, running her hands along the tops of every velvet bench until they'd reached their seat.

Soon, car number two was full—each row occupied by two passengers. Most were either teenagers or adults, and Molly and Noah started to realize they were the only kids in sight. A few nosy passengers gave Noah and Molly a look, but for the most part everybody seemed to be in their own world.

Just when Molly started to relax, the sound of static burst through speakers somewhere on the wall. *"Attention ladies and gentleman. The Night Train will depart in thirty seconds. Everyone please take his or her seat."*

Anyone still standing quickly slid into a

bench, and the passengers waited in the silence, anticipating the beginning of what was bound to be an exciting adventure. Lights faded as a rush of gauzy, smoky mist seeped up from the floor, slithering through the passengers like a coil of snakes.

The train pulled forward, slowly picking up speed.

Molly stared out the glass-domed roof as vivid patterns in the tiled ceiling blurred into streaks of color. The smooth sound of the engine pulled her into a trance. She was mesmerized by the smell of polished floors, the spooky mist floating through the cabin, and the swirling colors chasing her through the glass-domed roof above.

They were thrown into darkness again, broken only briefly as bright lights flashed on and off outside the train like streaks of lightening.

Heads turned left and right, all trying to see out the window, trying to guess what might come next. Bursts of colorful lights ignited throughout the car, fading from mustard yellow to deep purple to a bright, neon pink.

The brass doors at the front and back of each car suddenly slid open, releasing a string of acrobats dressed head to toe in gold leotards.

They shot down the aisle, flipping backward and forward…backward and forward, flying by so fast they were soon just a sparkly blur of gold.

After the last acrobat disappeared, the colored lights and smoke faded, leaving the cabin bathed in darkness as the train burst forth from the tunnel, out into the open sky. Through the domed roof, Molly looked up to find a clear, starry night.

"Welcome to the Night Train," spoke a deep, soothing voice through the intercom. *"We are certain you will enjoy your ride with us tonight on our 1952 5-car Pullman Dome Train."*

The announcer continued, but Molly couldn't help from tuning him out. She really didn't care about how the train was built or when and why it was converted from a freight train to a passenger train. She was just excited to be on board!

After ten or so minutes, the train slowed, flattening everyone into their seat as it started up a steep incline. Molly held her breath and clutched the seat cushion, ready to scream at the slightest indication of any type of nosedive.

It was coming…*she knew it*…any second they would plunge *straight down…*

Any second now…

But, instead of shooting downward like she

expected, the train swung hard to the left and then leveled out before continuing forward.

Huh.

Molly's big breath fizzled out, and she unclenched her hands.

Another announcement echoed through the car: *"Our next attraction will be on your left in approximately five minutes. In the meantime, lean backward, look upward, and enjoy our special star-gazing show."*

She looked around, wondering if everybody was following the announcer's directions. Apparently so—it appeared she was the only one not staring up through the glass at the starry sky above. Even Noah.

What a bunch of conformers.

A hypnotic melody played through the loudspeakers, but Molly couldn't see what all the fuss was about; it was just a dark sky filled with a bunch of stars that were much too far away.

"Whoa...this is so cool," said Noah.

Molly turned to see him staring out the glass like he was watching the most interesting video game ever. His arms and legs were long and loose, making Molly wonder why it was so hard for her to stop thinking about everything for two minutes and just enjoy looking at a star for once, like Noah.

She tried imitating his positioning—shoulders lowered, hips halfway down the seat, and legs slightly bent. But, it felt funny being all slouchy like that, and she still couldn't clear her mind.

The music stopped.

And so had the train.

Ooohs and *Aahhhs* filled the car.

"Check it out," Noah said.

Molly opened her eyes, wondering what the big deal was. But, when she looked out the window, she understood. And she sat up straight.

From every window she could see across the bay, to the city skyline flickering with a million glowing lights, to the outline of the bridge. Behind that, the horizon hinted at tree-topped hills covered in oozy, marshmallowy fog. Molly felt like she was at the top of the world, halfway to the moon.

Until she caught a glimpse of Bell's Bluff prison's dark outline far down below, carved into the cliffs of Blue Rock Island, all alone and abandoned like a haunted house.

She stood up, pressing her hands against the window, her breath forming clouds on the glass. People were standing now, too, trying to get a better view like Molly. She could hear quiet conversations of passengers pointing out places and naming landmarks. But her eyes seemed forever stuck on Bell's Bluff. She had never seen it from this angle, where everything felt so up close and personal.

It almost seemed...*alive.*

"Hey, you okay?" Noah asked.

Molly offered him a weak smile and sank back down into her seat, trying not to dwell anymore on thoughts of the prison so she could enjoy the rest of the train ride. Somehow it had dampened her spirits, even here on the Night Train with her best friend by her side.

A bank of overhead lights ignited above them, lighting every cabin from the inside to a dim, moody yellow. Molly's heart sunk even further. *Was the ride over already?*

"Menu, Ma'am?"

Molly turned to find a dark-haired lady with chocolate skin and blood red lipstick beside her bench. She held out a digital tablet.

Molly wasn't especially hungry. But, she was so relieved the ride wasn't over that she happily grabbed the tablet. The second her fingers touched the screen, a list of food items with accompanying photos appeared on the screen. Molly scrolled down, and the list kept going and going and going...

Finally, she stopped, overwhelmed at the

possibilities.

How was she supposed to choose anything? Not only that, but she'd neglected to bring her wallet, too. Talk about embarrassing. Now everyone else would enjoy all the food they wanted, leaving Noah and Molly looking like poor, sorry orphan kids.

"You don't have any cash on you, do you?" she side-whispered to Noah, hoping nobody else could hear.

"I don't think it costs anything." Noah pointed to the top corner of his menu.

"Why do you say that?"

"Look up here. It says, *'Compliments of The Night Train.'* Doesn't that sound like it's free to you?"

Molly thought for a minute, wondering if maybe Noah had a point. She then scrolled through the never-ending list of food items again, searching for dollar signs. But, it appeared Noah was on to something again.
The entire menu was dollar-sign-free!

Which made it very easy to order.

A half-hour later, people were starting to stare. Molly couldn't help it that the menu had so many delicious options.

"I told you we ordered way too much," Noah said under his breath, not looking her directly in the eye.

"You'll thank me later," she said, pushing a long spoon into a caramel-smothered ice cream sundae. It was one of many desserts piled onto a silver platter that had popped up from the backside of the bench in front of them.

At first, a plate of warm chocolate chip cookies and two tall, frosty glasses of milk seemed like a good start. But then Molly couldn't chase the image from her mind of the chocolate banana cream pie, which was when Noah mentioned he'd never tried frozen chocolate-covered bananas and they'd always sounded good. Molly started feeling sorry for him because who hasn't had a frozen chocolate-covered banana by the time they are twelve? So, she ordered two.

And then it just snowballed from there.

Molly supposed they should have ordered like every other passenger in the car—maybe a hamburger and a shake, or steak and potatoes and a slice of chocolate cake. But when you run into a menu that tells you to please order whatever you like because it's free, then why apply self-imposed rules that limit your possibilities?

It just made no sense!

Plus, Molly could tell Noah was secretly

happy to have such a giant assortment of desserts and junk food in front of him, especially because his parents were always eating Lean Cuisines and green shakes with stuff like spinach and carrots in them.

Now their tray was overflowing with sweets. Even carrot cake, which Molly didn't like at all, but she thought—*why not?*

When the attendant brought them a third round of desserts—this time a delicious collection of cheesecakes and tarts, she finally gave Molly and Noah the frown Molly had been anticipating for some time.

Molly ignored it.

It wasn't until she was in the middle of a root beer float cupcake that Molly's stomach finally seemed to register she'd had enough. It was a sad moment—one she never thought she'd ever have in her life.

Slowly, she separated the partially eaten cupcake from her mouth and put it on the tray. "Ugh. I'm stuffed."

"Me too," said Noah, rubbing his stomach.

While an attendant cleared off the overflowing tray of food, Molly leaned back against the cushioned bench, wishing her stomach didn't look and feel like a bulging water balloon.

Moments before her eyelids surrendered to her food coma, a small, white object hit her leg just as a long-haired man with suspiciously dark sunglasses passed by her bench.

"Hey, what was that?" Noah asked.

Molly looked down to find a small square of paper folded into fours lying in her lap. She picked it up and unfolded the paper, wondering what, if anything, was written inside.

That was when the lights went out.

CHAPTER 19

California Screamin'

"Ladies and Gentlemen. We hope you enjoyed your spectacular dining experience at the top of Blue Rock Island—the only place in the world with 360˚ views of the bay, as well as a birds-eye view of Bell's Bluff, California's oldest federal penitentiary."

A cloud of fog seeped up from the floor and the train jerked forward. Too curious to wait for better lighting, Molly slid out of her seat and knelt on the floor, where she held the tiny piece of paper up to a speck of light at the base of her seat.

It read: **Car 4 Row 8.**

She hopped back in her seat and whispered the message to Noah.

"What do you think it means?" he asked.

"I don't know. Do you think the man dropped it on purpose? Or was it just a coincidence? Or was he trying to send a message to someone else, and I intercepted it?"

"How should I know?"

"Maybe I should go to car four and check it out. Just in case."

"You mean, right now?"

The train was accelerating.

"Why not?" Molly said. "It shouldn't take very long."

"And now, for the next leg of our adventure— what some would call a criminally wild ride."

Molly slid out into the aisle, but Noah pulled her back down beside him.

"What?" she asked.

"I don't think you're supposed to just get up and walk around in the middle of the ride," he said, a worried look on his face.

Molly looked around the car. "Well, who's going to stop me? It's not like they read us a bunch of rules or anything."

"I know. But, I don't want you to get in trouble."

Molly yanked free of Noah's grasp and stood up again. "Relax, Noah. Who's going to get me in trouble? And, what could they do to me anyway?

Put me out on the caboose til the end of time?"

Noah's grimace loosened into an easy smile, and the muscles in his neck and shoulders relaxed at the thought of Molly being stuck outside on the tail end of the train. He loved how she could make everything into a joke...even if it was soaked in hyperbole.

He still couldn't help being nervous, though, when she walked away from him. But, at least she was smiling.

Molly headed straight for the brass doors, wondering what she might find in car four, row eight.

The announcer started talking again, but Molly was so focused on reaching car number four that she completely tuned out. She pushed through the sliding doors, and found herself stuck for a moment between the cars. Surprisingly, she found that she liked it there in that little compartment where it was just her and nobody else—no announcer, no long-haired man, no jazzy piano music or glass roof.

Just Molly.

But she knew she had to keep moving, especially now that the train felt like it was accelerating. She wasn't sure how much more time she had before something positively spectacular happened, and didn't want to miss out on a one-of-a-kind Night Train experience because she'd gone exploring in the middle of it.

In the next car she took a deep breath and gripped the handrails. Car number three was identical to car number two, and as Molly made her way down the aisle, she wondered why it felt like the train was tilting downwards.

The announcer started talking again.

Molly stumbled forward and pushed through the next set of brass doors into car number four. Row eight was empty, which seemed strange, considering every other row was filled with passengers.

She walked down the aisle and slid into row number eight like she belonged there, and found a large, flat cardboard box just sitting there all by itself. Molly looked around for nosy passengers, and then lifted the lid.

Inside was an envelope like the one she'd found in her mailbox this morning. But it was too dark inside the car to read anything at the moment, so Molly thought it best to return to her own seat and wait for more light.

With the card tucked into her pocket, she left the box on the seat and stepped into the aisle. Just then, the train dipped forward, causing Molly to lose her balance and fall on the floor.

The combination of momentum and gravity

meant there was little Molly could do but lay sprawled on her back and gape at the starry-night glass above her as the train plunged downward like a rollercoaster.

She reached for anything she could to brace herself and keep from tumbling like a bowling ball all the way down the aisle, which ended up being a scrawny leg on her right and the bench on her left.

When the train finally leveled out, Molly's heart somehow crawled its way back to her chest and hid there. Her fingers ached. The scrawny leg in her grasp jerked free. But, it still seemed Molly couldn't move; she'd been molded onto the floor like a flattened piece of dough pressed into the bottom of a pie pan.

At last she released the foot of the bench, and came to her knees just as the next announcement sounded over the loudspeaker. *"Ladies and Gentlemen of the Night Train. We have reached the next stop on our tour and ask that you remain seated until the car doors on the left of the train slide open."*

Molly worried about Noah. He was probably wondering what had happened to her, probably having a panic attack this very moment.

"Please take any valuables with you, as the Night Train cannot be responsible for any lost or

stolen items."

She pulled herself up from the floor at the steady hum of conversation between the passengers. It seemed they were trying not to stare, though Molly could tell they were having a hard time not looking at her. She couldn't blame them, though, but still wished they'd mind their own business. It wasn't her fault the train ride had turned into a rollercoaster in the middle of her sleuthing.

After dusting off her sweatpants and checking her pocket to make sure she hadn't lost the envelope, Molly pushed her way through the passengers all lining up behind the doors.

At the back of the car, she slid the brass doors open and stepped through, not realizing until it was too late that she had walked right into Officer Wolfe.

CHAPTER
20

New Fears and Nightmares

Molly didn't know what to say. Officer Wolfe seemed just as surprised to see her, as she was to see him.

"Excuse me," she finally said, maneuvering around his tall, overbearing form, wondering what *he* was doing here? What a buzz-kill. First he'd ruined her doughnut outing, and now her train ride, too?

Officer Wolfe grunted something under his breath, and to Molly's relief, made his own escape into car number four without saying anything uncomfortable or out of order.

On the other side of the brass doors, Molly breathed a sigh of relief. She found an empty spot up against the wall, and waited there to catch her breath. After that rollercoaster plunge and then coming face to face with one of her least favorite people in the world, Molly could sense all that food in her stomach growing restless.

The train doors to her left slid open to a cool, breezy night. The sudden blast of salty air calmed her. She closed her eyes as the passengers began to file out of the train, into the darkness.

"There you are," said a familiar voice.

Molly opened her eyes to find Noah weaving his way toward her.

"Are you okay?" he asked once he reached her.

Her heart warmed at his presence, and she nodded, yes, thinking that *now* she was just fine.

Molly waited until after they had disembarked with the rest of the passengers to show Noah the letter she'd found. Unfortunately, the moment they stepped off the train, it was much too dark to see the space in front of them, much less a message inside an envelope. She would have to wait until they could find a little light to open it up.

The moon hung low over the island, its bright belly partially hidden behind fat, dark shapes. Molly contemplated the still, dark space surrounding them, realizing too soon that nothing looked familiar. In fact, she had been too busy trying not to roll down the aisle that she hadn't even heard the announcement indicating their location or a purpose for disembarking.

She stopped and looked around, trying to make sense of the hazy shapes hunkering in the distance. The familiar sound of ebbing and flowing waves, and the heavy scent of salty, soggy wood of waterlogged boards let her know they were down by the shore. You get used to certain smells when you live on an island.

But it was as black as mud out there, and other than the moon's soft glow illuminating the bay, Molly couldn't see much of anything as they walked single file along a wooden boardwalk, away from the water.

"Where are we, anyway?" asked Molly, still trying to catch her breath.

"You didn't hear the announcer?"

She shook her head, wondering why Noah sounded so surprised.

"Bell's Bluff," he said, as if that was the most obvious thing in the world.

"We're—WHERE?"

The man in front of them paused at Molly's outburst.

Oh my goodness… "WHY are we at Bell's Bluff?" Molly strangled Noah's arm. "What are we doing at the most dangerous, freaky prison in the country, *in the middle of the night?*"

"Calm down," said Noah, shaking loose from her death grip. "We don't have to keep going if you don't want to. I'm sure we can sit on the train and wait until it's time to go again. Remember, this is your adventure, not mine."

"I know…I know…" She shivered, considering Noah's words, trying to understand what it was about Bell's Bluff that bothered her so much.

What it came down to, she decided, was simple. Bell's Bluff signified murder and dying and death—all things that belonged in nightmares—and the exact kind of things that had no place in any adventure of hers.

Wasn't Noah supposed to be the scared one, anyway? Molly searched his eyes for that same fear she'd seen earlier at the top of Candlestick Hill, but all she could find was the glowing, orbed reflection of the moon. Wasn't *she* the brave one? Didn't she just prove her bravery only an hour ago, when she had to convince Noah to follow her down the trapdoor stairs? Now he didn't look scared, not even a little bit—and the idea that *she* was the scared one didn't sit well with her. Not at all.

It's just an old, deserted prison, she reasoned under her breath, trying to shake loose the uneasy feeling rolling around in her gut.

Except, all the talk over the years about escaped convicts being eaten by sharks was starting to get to Molly, especially after seeing the poster earlier today at the doughnut shop. Almost like Bell's Bluff was screaming for her attention. Everything about this seemed too coincidental...like a premonition of something horrible to come.

"Do you want to go back on the train?" Noah whispered in Molly's ear so nobody else would hear. She was grateful to him for that.

"No..." She shook her head, not willing to admit how terrified she was as they continued along the boardwalk with the rest of the passengers. "It's okay," she said, trying to convince herself, as well as him. She didn't feel exactly right inside, but wasn't going to let her fear of Bell's Bluff get in the way of her adventure, even if she had to hold her breath the whole way through it.

A hum of whispers filled the air, a crescendo of chatter and even concern in anticipation of whatever might happen next. Molly did not share in the fervor, but remained leery as the train

117

passengers waited there in the dark, knowing...*feeling* that something was about to happen. Any second.

Pop!

It happened.

A mixture of lights and noises and music came to life like one giant pop of a light bulb. The whole crowd stopped, everyone oohing and awing at the sight in front of them, followed by loud clapping and cheering, and then running toward the lights.

CHAPTER
21

The long haired-man with the dark sunglasses exited first, ambling in the dark up the wood-planked walkway before the rest of the passengers filed out. He would stay hidden in the shadows and observe from there.

But he didn't know who to keep his eye on the most—Molly Pepper and her companion, or the FBI agents disembarking this very second. He'd been assigned to follow them both; but he had his preference.

After dropping the clue, he slunk into the rear seat of car number two and waited for Molly's curiosity to get the best of her, which it did. Of course it did. He'd watched her head down the aisle and disappear through the brass doors. When the rollercoaster hit and she hadn't returned, he couldn't help feeling a little nervous. But then again, how far could she go on a four-car train?

He found her with Noah in car number three. He could tell by the look on her face that she'd found the note.

That was the most important thing.

CHAPTER 22

Wishes and Fireflies

The first thing to catch Molly's eye was a Ferris wheel in the distance, propped up against the moon on a small hill. It spun through the sky, filling the night with dancing lights, like a giant kaleidoscope, reminding Molly of another day...

She and her mother had been snuggled together in bed. It was after her mother's hair had grown back curly. Molly liked to hold the strands between her fingers, while her mother reminisced from when she was a little girl, back when she lived in Chicago, home to the biggest Ferris wheel ever made.

"It sits at the edge of the dock, out over the pier, so all the lights reflect into the water, just like fireflies," she'd said, tickling Molly's arm.

"What are fireflies?" Molly asked.

Her mom's eyes blinked wide in surprise. "You've never seen a firefly before?"

"I don't think so."

She sighed. Whenever her mom sighed, it meant she was thinking.

So, Molly waited.

Finally. "I'll take you. One of these days we'll fly to Chicago in the summertime, and we'll eat cotton candy and ride the Ferris wheel and chase fireflies until we catch one."

It sounded like a fabulous idea. She smiled at the thought of it. "Promise?"

Her mother squeezed her arm. "Promise," she said, coughing.

Molly thought she heard a creak on the floorboard as her mother's bedroom door inched open. Molly looked up, expecting to see Dad standing in the doorway, wiping his eyes and wanting to join them, too. But there was no one there.

When Molly turned back, eager for more stories and bigger promises, her mother's eyes had already closed. Her breathing was soft. And quiet. Molly laid her head on her chest and fell asleep to the sound of her heart.

Still beating.

Now, under a starry sky, Molly turned to Noah, knowing exactly where she wanted to go. "I need to ride that Ferris wheel," she said as her earlier sense of dread faded a little at the image of her mother behind her eyes.

"Let's go, then." Noah smiled.

The small crowd began to thin out, the train passengers splitting off in different directions. Molly wondered how everyone could be so at ease and willing to venture far from the train. This was still a prison, after all.

Didn't anybody know that?

They stopped first at a wooden gate beneath what seemed to be the official entrance to the carnival. An arched sign made of rough, planked boards stretched from left to right above their heads, covered in big bold letters.

MIDNIGHT CARNIVAL

"Carnival," Molly repeated, loving the way the word sounded on her tongue. "I've never been to a carnival before. Have you?"

"Not this late, that's for sure."

Just past the Carnival sign, two long rows of booths with black and gold awnings faced each other like a neat line of soldiers. Each booth showed off its own old-fashioned game: ring tossing, target practice with old-fashioned guns, fish bowl toss, balloon darts —even a dunk tank holding a skinny man who shivered against the cool air in a pair of measly swim trunks. Water streamed down his face, all the way to his toes.

Around the corner from the dripping man, a little further up the pathway stood a steeply peaked tent that was as tall as a tree. Inside, covering the shelves was every kind of treat a kid could ever want—at least *these* kids. Molly wandered up to the tent, amazed at the assortment in front of her, wishing she hadn't stuffed her face earlier on the train.

In the very front of the display were fluffy tufts of cotton candy, giant boxes of movie-theater style candy, including Molly's very favorite (cinnamon bears), and big pink and white striped candy sticks wrapped in cellophane. Beneath that, giant tubs of ice cream lined a long row inside a freezer, each one filled to the top with a different flavor. A glass case as tall as the man standing beside it was filled with popcorn popping a tornado of yellow and white, and above that, sitting on a ledge and ready for tasters, were thick rows of different colored fudge resting on little squares of waxed paper.

"Can I help you?" asked a red-haired man nearly hidden behind a wispy, peppery mustache. He seemed friendly enough in his puffy white shirt with oversized sleeves tucked into a black vest.

Molly observed the display, trying to find a sign with the names of the treats or their prices. But the booth was sign-free.

"How much is the cotton candy?" she asked. Even though she was stuffed, she decided that a bite of cotton candy was like swallowing something the size of a breath mint by the time everything dissolved in her mouth. *That*, she could manage.

"How much? Why, it's courtesy of The Night Train, of course!" the man laughed, throwing his arms out to either side of him.

Of course, Molly thought, still unable to make sense of this whole 'free' business. Tonight she wished her stomach were a lot bigger! Still, she couldn't resist scooping up a handful of cinnamon bears and putting them in her pocket, just in case she needed a snack or a pick-me-up a little later.

Noah strolled up to the booth and helped himself to a box of Junior Mints. "Thanks," he said, glancing up at the booth worker.

"Enjoy your time at the Carnival," he said, still smiling.

Molly contemplated the cotton candy, but

decided it wasn't worth throwing up over, even if it *did* only take up a millimeter inside her stomach.

"Come on," Noah said, heading past the candy booth and further into the carnival grounds.

They wandered up the pebbly pathway, through various booths and attractions, peeking into a few gold and black striped tents. But they decided not to linger at any of them—the line at the tent belonging to a fortune-teller was much too long, and a magician in the other tent was on the verge of revealing something big; Molly figured it would be rude to barge in and ruin his momentum.

After dodging a glittery-faced woman with two white braids, juggling seven soda cans, Molly stopped under a tall, black lamppost shooting down an eerie ray of green light.

"Why are we stopping?" asked Noah.

"The note." Molly remembered, bringing the envelope into the light.

"Do you think it was meant for you?" he asked. "Or, did you intercept somebody else's secret message?"

"How should I know?"

"Well, what does it say?"

They crowded into the same lamp lit space,

their heads bumping into each other as Molly opened the envelope and pulled out the card. Squinting under the garish, dim light Molly and Noah read aloud the words printed on the card: **COME FLY WITH ME IN NUMBER 3.**

Molly looked up. "Come fly with me? How are we supposed to do that?"

"I don't think it's being literal."

"I know that. I'm just saying—"

Out of the shadows darted a string of people, dancing and laughing and turning in circles. They all covered their faces with fancy, sequined masks as a little man danced an Irish jig around them, strumming on a miniature guitar.

And then, as fast as they had arrived, everybody dispersed into five different directions like the fading sparkler from a firecracker.

"What was that?" asked Molly.

"Weird. That's what it was," said Noah, taking the note from Molly and reading the clue one more time.

"Let's keep going," said Molly when she realized she could hear the sound of big band music spilling down the hill toward them. It seemed to originate from the spinning lights of the Ferris wheel, like a siren song, as if trying to draw her up there. And it worked. Molly couldn't resist—not with the memory of her mother or the big band music that made her want to dance or the alluring appeal of the sparkly perimeter lights lighting up the top of the hill.

Noah gave the note back to Molly. She tucked it into her pocket as they left their circle of lamplight and headed up the hill, past the remaining black and gold booths. With the Ferris wheel within reach now, it was easy to ignore the other booths filled with candy and cheap animals stuffed too full; Molly had one prize in mind, and it had nothing to do with an oversized elephant.

That was, until halfway up the hill, just past the gold and black striped tents, something sparkly caught her attention, drawing her away from the pebbly path. Noah followed her as she crept forward through the rocks, unable to take her eyes off what looked like a ceiling of twinkling stars hanging from a cluster of trees.

"What is it?" asked Molly.

Two Cypress trees stretched high into the sky, their branches leaning hard to the left like bony witches' fingers trying to escape the wind. From their branches draped long rows of string, crisscrossing back and forth from tree to tree, the string holding up a handful of glowing glass jars.

When Molly caught sight of the jars, she ran forward in an attempt to unhook a jar from the line. But it seemed stuck, no matter how hard she tugged. She moved on to another jar, hoping for better luck with that one, and then another.

"You got to make a wish, there."

Molly jumped backward, trying to find a face belonging to the deep, growly voice heavy with an Irish accent. Her eyes took a minute to adjust from the lights above to the shadows below where an old man sat on the ground under the jars. He was leaning backward against the wide trunk of one of the trees. A little patch of white hair covered his head, and his face crawled with white, scruffy whiskers. The rest of his body was hidden in the shadows.

"A wish? You mean, like a birthday wish?" Molly asked.

The man rose to his feet, edging a little further into the light. Even standing, he hunched over so much that he didn't look much taller than Molly.

"No. Not like a birthday wish at all," he said, ending his sentence in an up note, as if asking a question, himself. His accent reminded Molly of leprechauns and pots of gold.

"What's inside the jars?" she asked.

"Fireflies," the man said, gazing up at the

canopy of glowing jars, like he could possibly be more in awe of them than she was.

Not a chance.

"Why do I have to make a wish to get one?" she asked, staring up, mesmerized. "Can't you just give it to me like the rest of the stuff they give out here for free?"

The man laughed, until something caught in his throat and brought up a cough. "Do you have any idea how long it took me to fill each one of these jars with *that* many fireflies?" he asked.

Molly shook her head, wondering where you go to catch fireflies.

"Well, then—since I'm the one who did all the catching, don't you think I should be able to decide who gets to take one?"

"I guess so. But if you care so much, why don't you just charge money?"

"Because my employer dictates that no exchange of money is allowed on Carnival Night. But nobody said anything about exchange of wishes," he said, chuckling again.

"What kind of wish are you looking for, if you don't want the regular ol' birthday wish?" Noah asked.

Molly added, "Yeah. I have a lot of birthday wishes stored up in my memory that have yet to come true. They could all use a second chance."

"Did I already ask if you had any idea how long it took me to catch every one of those fireflies?"

"Yep." Molly nodded, wondering if his memory was a little hard to catch, too.

"Wishes aren't easy, either," Noah responded boldly. "Real wishes, at least."

What did Noah know about wishes?

The old man laughed again. "I think you're onto something, kid," he said, patting Noah on the shoulder.

Molly closed her eyes and ran through her long list of unfulfilled wishes, trying to force her own silent wishes to somehow turn into magic and make themselves known to the firefly man. But all Molly could do was stare at him as he stood in front of her, arms folded. Something seemed so familiar about him—something in his eyes.

She drew closer for a better look, but he turned his head away from her, like she was getting too close.

At that moment, Molly decided the firefly man was talking about something other than fireflies and wishes, and she wanted to ask him what he meant by her very best wish. "Wait," Molly said, trying to follow him.

Noah pulled her back. "You're not supposed

to follow him," he whispered, as if there was a rule about following firefly men.

It didn't matter, though. The firefly man had been sucked into the shadows, leaving Noah and Molly alone beneath his firefly jars without a way for Molly to keep one for herself.

CHAPTER 23

Come Fly With Me

Reluctantly, Molly left with Noah and headed to the Ferris wheel, hopeful to find her spirits lifted there. If she couldn't get her own firefly jar, well at least maybe her very first ride on a Ferris wheel would make up for it.

As they approached the big, spinning wheel, the music grew louder and louder, the lights brighter and brighter. They stopped at the base of it, gazing up at the giant rotating wheel, its twinkling lights brightening the sky. The wooden cars rocked back and forth as the wheel turned, reminding Molly of her mother.

It had been four months since she last saw her. Four months and eleven days.

Boy, did she miss her.

Molly needed a cinnamon bear. Now. She fished one out of her pocket and shoved it in her mouth. The second the hot sting of the gooey candy squished between her teeth, she felt a little more at ease…a little less melancholy.

"Can you believe this thing?"

Molly jumped at the sound of Noah's voice in her ear as something like sadness seemed to stick in her throat. She coughed and attempted a smile, even though the opposite of happy was pulling at her mouth. After blinking enough times to scare away any threatening tears, she took a deep breath. "Are you ready?" she asked.

"Let's go," Noah said, leading the way up the pathway to the roped entrance of the ride. Eight others were already there, waiting in line for a turn. It seemed most of the other train passengers were gathered around the black and gold-capped booths down the hill, probably winning prizes and still stuffing their faces with goodies.

The wheel had come to a stop now, and the operator was rotating the cars into place, one by one. Music coming from the Ferris wheel speakers drowned out everything else in the background—an old fashioned kind of song with horns and drums and a swingy beat.

"I love this song," said Noah with a big smile.

"Frank Sinatra is my Dad's favorite singer."

"Frank—*who?*" Molly asked, enjoying the taste of cinnamon lingering in her mouth.

Noah frowned. "*Sinatra.* You don't know who Frank Sinatra is?"

"Nope. But it does sound kind of familiar," Molly said, her shoulders and legs moving along with the beat as the singer belted out something about floating down Peru and llamas... *Llamas?*

Noah grabbed Molly's arm, jerking her toward him. "The song!" he said loud enough to garner a few strange looks from their fellow future Ferris wheel passengers.

Noah lowered his voice. "Do you hear the song?"

"I wasn't really listening to the words. Mostly just enjoying the beat."

"Well, listen again. You'll get it."

Molly wondered why Noah's smile was so big as she waited for the singer to break into song again after the little music interlude. When his voice started up, she first heard something about birds, a honeymoon and Acapulco Bay, which she thought sounded a little too lovey-dovey for her. She almost told Noah she didn't know what he was talking about...but, then she heard it, too: "*Come Fly With Me, Let's fly, let's fly...Let's fly away!*"

Come fly with me in car number 3.

Molly felt her smile matching Noah's as they reached the front of the line. She wasn't sure how to insist on being placed into car number 3, but it turned out she didn't even have to worry. The empty car waiting for them was already marked number 3.

A very strange coincidence, thought Molly.

The Ferris wheel car was a little wobbly, and Molly and Noah waited at the top of the platform until the operator had stepped out of his booth and shuffled up the steps to assist them. He wore a black hat and black and gold striped vest with white, poofy sleeves like the rest of the Carnival workers, though his face and head sprouted black hair from just about everywhere a piece of hair can sprout.

Like a Wolfman.

"You'll have to wait a minute while I turn the crank, if you don't mind," he said, his voice a little scratchy-sounding, just how Molly imagined a werewolf might sound.

The other people in front who had just settled into their own car sighed, like the Ferris wheel man had really put a cramp in their style. Molly wanted to tell them to relax. It wasn't like they were about to ride a Ferris wheel in the middle of the night, or something outrageous like that. *Sheesh.* Maybe they could use a cinnamon bear of their own. But, Molly wasn't offering up any of hers.

After the Ferris wheel man pushed a few buttons and pulled on a long, red lever in the controller booth, at last car number 3 was ready for Noah and Molly to climb aboard.

Noah let Molly step inside first, and then quickly took his own seat opposite her, so they were facing each other.

The brassy music streamed from speakers somewhere inside the car, making Molly realize she was really starting to like this Frank Sinatra guy. And not just because his lyrics had something to do with her adventure.

The operator kept his head down as he fumbled with the lock on the gate. Molly peered down at his hands, all tanned and wrinkled and covered in knuckles. Just before he stepped away from the car, she caught a glimpse of the number thirteen tattooed on his left index finger. It seemed familiar to her, like a déjà vu, the image of the number 13— a repeat.

Was it?

Molly settled into her seat when the sound of a familiar voice bounded up toward them from down below. "...sure you saw them get on?" said the deep voice approaching the base of the Ferris wheel platform. "I don't see them anywhere."

"Listen…" Molly whispered to Noah.

"Yes, I'm sure!" said another, this one a little higher pitched, though not much. "Plus, that's what that hippie told us."

Molly and Noah leaned over the edge of the car. Sure enough, twelve feet below, just stepping into the light was the top of Officer Wolfe's dark head, the bridge of his nose protruding far beyond his face. He appeared to be in an argument with a short, stocky older woman.

Molly frowned. What was Officer Wolfe doing here, too? It seemed that lately everywhere she went, he happened to be there, just trying to ruin her life.

"I don't see her anywhere, is all I'm saying," said Officer Wolfe.

"How did you lose track of her so easily? It was a simple job."

Noah and Molly ducked their heads inside the car and held as still as possible. Noah seemed just as shocked as Molly, but looked much more terrified with his eyes bugged-out like two flying saucers.

"It wasn't my fault we got stuck in the middle of those stupid dancing masks and that Irish fiddler!"

"This better be the spot Molly Pepper is meeting up with Moody," Officer Wolfe's lady friend continued, "Or your job's on the line. I'm getting sick of all your excuses."

Molly could hear the woman's voice very clearly, and couldn't help but jerk upright when she heard her name. How could this woman possibly know Molly was meeting up with somebody—when Molly didn't even know it herself? And why was Officer Wolfe so nosy and up in her business all day long?

Molly inched her head over the edge of the car even further, trying to figure out what they were talking about. The Ferris wheel operator cranked the car forward until car number 4 was in position. He opened the door for the next customers as they stepped into the teetering car.

"Why are you so confident she's meeting up with him, Ruby?" asked Officer Wolfe.

"Think about it. She's at Bell's Bluff on June 13th, which just so happens to be his anniversary. I'm telling you, Moody is finally making his move, and the girl will lead us right to him. If you don't lose track of her again, that is."

The Ferris wheel operator turned and descended the stairs until he was face to face with Officer Wolfe and Ruby Dodd. "Welcome to the Ferris wheel," he said, smiling underneath that face full of hair. Are you planning on joining us, or shall we continue without you?"

"I don't know…" Ruby lifted her head upward for a better view of the lighted wheel before Molly had a chance to duck.

Molly knew she'd been discovered the second she saw the delighted look on Ruby's face. "Shoot!" whispered Molly, sliding back into her seat a few seconds too late. There was nothing she could do about it now.

Noah's face went white. "She saw us! What are we going to do?"

They were stuck, really. Already lifted up above the platform, they had no other choice but to remain in their seats and see what unfolded now. The idea of being trapped didn't sit well with Molly, and Noah looked like he might lose his recently devoured Junior Mints.

"On second thought, I think we'll have a ride, after all," they heard Ruby say, a bounce of confidence in her voice.

Noah slunk further into the wooden bench.

Molly's heart sank. She worried her Ferris wheel ride would be completely ruined now.

"Step right up to the platform, and I'll get you situated," said the Ferris wheel operator.

Molly chewed on another cinnamon bear and then leaned over the edge of the wobbly car again, figuring she might as well keep an eye on the action down below, now that she'd been discovered. Ruby and Wolfe were climbing up the creaking stairs.

"Who's *Moody?*" asked Noah.

Molly thought that name sounded a little familiar, herself, but couldn't quite pinpoint why. "I don't know."

Ruby and Wolfe stepped into the car two cars behind theirs, and as soon as Wolfe was seated, his black, BB-eyes lifted to meet Molly's.

He smiled.

Molly almost looked away, intimidated by those dark, deep-set eyes. But the anger she'd felt toward him earlier today in the doughnut shop came rushing back at the thought of Officer Wolfe deliberately ruining her Ferris wheel ride, and for the first time in her life Molly felt like punching somebody.

If only they weren't separated by a twenty-foot span of air, she was certain she would really do it. Her fists were already clamped down into little balls, just looking for a target. And that big nose looked like a bull's eye to her.

"Molly!" Noah was tugging at Molly's arm, his sudden movement swinging the car back and forth. She fell backward in her seat and gripped the edges of the car.

"What?" she asked, trying to find Noah.

The Ferris wheel had started rotating upward, their car slowing lifting. Before it had lifted too far off the ground, Molly and Noah felt a sudden lurch beneath them. They gaped over the edge of their car to find the Ferris wheel operator dangling from the edge while the wheel still turned.

What was he doing? Molly jumped backward, not knowing what to do about their car being hijacked. Maybe the Ferris wheel operator was a Russian spy. He did have all that *hair…*

"Help him up!" yelled Noah, reaching over and pulling at the man's arm.

The man hefted himself up and found his footing on the outside ledge of the car. Molly fumbled with the lock, but it seemed stuck. She looked into the operator's face only inches from hers. He seemed so calm…something about those ocean blue eyes watching her.

The passengers in the other cars gaped in horror at the operator's bold move. Was he crazy? Had he lost his mind and was about to take over like a madman? Even Officer Wolfe and Ruby Dodd seemed as surprised as the rest of them.

But, then the man tumbled over the edge and

fell into the bottom of the car, a big smile on his face. In one swoop, he pulled a metal box out from underneath Molly's seat, and handed it to her.

Wolfe and Ruby stood over the edge of their car as it swung back and forth in a giant arc. "It's him!" yelled Ruby, pointing at Molly and Noah's car.

Him? Who, *him?* Molly wondered.

Molly faced the Ferris wheel operator, wondering what on earth he was doing here. First Officer Wolfe had crashed their party, and now a strange werewolf man from Russia had decided to be a party-crasher, too. What was going on?

"Are you okay, sir?" Noah asked, pulling him to his feet.

"Yes, I think so. Thank you."

The operator sat beside Noah, with his feet out in front of him. Molly still held onto the strange metal box, wondering what it was for.

The car lifted higher and higher as the wheel continued its rotation, Frank Sinatra belting in the background. Molly shifted her gaze from the strange metal box back to the man beside Noah, and held it there, as if demanding an explanation.

Instead of speaking, however, the man brought his hands to his face and started tugging at his skin. Molly's breath grew shallow and she felt her head go dizzy, certain the crazy Ferris wheel operator had started tearing his skin off.

Noah's eyes doubled in size, and a yelp clambered up his throat as he scrambled away from the man and leapt across the car to Molly's side, rocking their car all over again.

Between the rocking movement and the shock of the man tearing his face off, Molly almost lost her lunch. Except, when she looked up one more time to find out there was no blood underneath the torn-off skin. The Ferris wheel operator's face remained remarkably in tact underneath all that hair.

Molly tapped Noah's leg, begging him to see for himself.

Finally, he dared look just as the car rotated into a spot of moonlight.

All at once, the glow of silver moonlight hit the left side of the man's face, and Molly drew in a big breath. Sure enough, without the handlebar moustache, that big, bushy beard and a wave of jet-black hair, Molly realized the man sitting in front of her wasn't a Ferris wheel operator at all.

Noah gasped.

The Ferris wheel operator was Tom Flaky in disguise!

CHAPTER 24

Everything happened much too quickly for the long-haired man.

One second he was crouched behind a bush, watching the FBI agents board the Ferris wheel, and the next, there was a rush of movement followed by a chorus of shouting, and the Ferris wheel operator was straddling the outside of Molly's car.

The long-haired man's first instinct was to pull out his gun and demand the Ferris wheel operator step away from car number 3.

But, gut reaction wasn't always the best move. He'd learned this over the years, and so he waited, knowing his gun would always be there for backup.

It wasn't until he crept forward and hid

behind the controller booth to get a good look at the Ferris wheel operator's face, that he relaxed. Now he understood why he was instructed to make sure Ruby Dodd and Officer Wolfe knew that Molly Pepper was getting on the Ferris wheel.

It all made sense now.

The long-haired man remained in the shadows and watched everything unfold, wondering how in the world this was going to all go down.

Wondering how Molly Pepper would take the truth.

CHAPTER
25

The Night of Black and Gold

"Molly," Tom Flaky said, his deep, familiar voice booming toward her, all the scratchy hoarseness gone.

She could feel her own face flush with heat, and her hands go stiff. What was Tom Flaky doing here hijacking her Ferris wheel ride, wearing a werewolf man disguise?

"It's okay, Miss Molly," he said, reaching for her. "It's just me."

"I know," Molly said, letting him hold her freezing hands, but feeling confused, not knowing why he'd been wearing a disguise, not understanding what he was doing here.

The car shifted. Molly released Tom's hands and clutched the box in her lap as the Ferris wheel turned, lifting car number 3 to the highest point. The car holding Wolfe and Ruby was now two cars beneath them, but when Molly looked down, she could still see both of them leaning far out of their car and gazing upward, trying to get a better look at what was going on in car number 3.

"I suppose I have a little explaining to do," Tom chuckled, bringing Molly's attention back inside her own car.

Noah still seemed speechless. He continued to gape at werewolf man-turned-Tom Flaky as he gripped the edge of his seat, trying to make sense of the spectacle before his eyes. Molly, on the other hand, was already primed for questioning. "What's inside the box?" she asked.

"That's what I want to show you. But, let me explain a few things first."

"Good idea," Molly said as the Ferris wheel kept turning.

Tom pulled something resembling a walkie-talkie from his pocket, and turned a knob. The music blasting from the speakers grew louder and louder until every other noise had been blotted out, and all that could be heard now was the cool, smooth sound of Frank Sinatra's voice.

"First off, I'm sorry there wasn't a better place or time to tell you what I'm about to tell you," he said under the music, frowning. "We only have about..." Tom Flaky lifted his wrist to check the time. "...ten minutes, so you're going to hear the abbreviated version of the story."

"*What story?*"

"Let's begin at the starting point. Your mom."

"*My mom?* What does she have to do with this? My mom is gone, you know."

"That is the sad truth. But I did manage to see her one last time. Right before the end."

"You did?"

"Yes. I know about her promise she made to you."

"What promise?" Molly asked, though she knew exactly what promise he was talking about. It had something to do with fireflies and a Ferris wheel and a place called Chicago. But Molly had never voiced it out loud, and wasn't going to start now.

But, she still remembered.

Of course she did.

And, she wondered how Tom Flaky knew about it.

He continued. "Olivia always loved the Ferris wheel," he said, softly.

Olivia. Molly hadn't heard anybody else say her mother's first name in a long time.

Tom cleared his throat. "I'm not doing a very good job explaining, am I?"

She shook her head.

"Do you ever remember your mother telling you about her parents?"

"A little," Molly admitted. "But not much. Only that they died when she was little."

"Well...that's partially true."

Noah suddenly spoke up. "*Partially* true? What does that even mean?" he asked doubtfully, like all the other confusion hadn't quite been confusing enough until now.

Tom Flaky laughed. "I'm glad Molly has you for a friend. There's nothing more valuable than a loyal friend." Noah seemed to straighten up at that. "And, to answer your question—*yes,* your mother's mother died in childbirth. Olivia never knew her. Saddest day of my life."

His life?

Tom Flaky continued, "But your mother's *father* never died. He is still alive to this very day."

"He is?" Molly asked, shocked. "Then why did my mom tell me he was *dead?* And where is he?"

"Just like you, your mother grew up believing her father had died. That's what they told her. It was much easier to tell a ten-year-old that their father had died instead of telling her the truth."

"WHAT TRUTH?" Molly asked, leaning forward in her seat.

Tom Flaky paused. His eyes revealed something sad—something Molly had never noticed before. "When your mom was ten, her father was thrown into prison for something he didn't do," he said.

"Did they let him out?" Molly asked, still not quite sure if she was hearing things correctly. And how did people get put in jail unless they were guilty? Police didn't make mistakes, *did they?*

"Locked him up and threw away the key."

"He wasn't a *murderer*, was he?" Molly dared ask, though she was terrified of the truth. She couldn't stand it if her grandfather was a murderer.

Tom Flaky dodged the question with one of his own. "Did your mother tell you he was a magician?"

"Yes."

"His specialty was making things disappear."

"What kinds of things?" asked Noah.

"At first he tackled small objects, like shoes and hats and decks of cards. But over the years as he became more skilled, his illusions involved much more complicated subjects."

"Like, what?"

"Like living, breathing things...kittens, chickens, dogs. Even a horse, once."

"Whoa... I'd like to see that," said Noah.

Tom Flaky paused, as if waiting for the right words to come. Molly and Noah waited while the big band music played on.

"Soon your grandfather could make people disappear, too."

"No way," said Noah.

Molly gulped, feeling a tingle scurry up her arms.

"But on the night of his greatest performance—*The Night of Black and Gold,* it was called, underneath a tall black tent on a stage in front of four hundred people—your grandfather made the mayor of Chicago disappear."

Molly's eyes felt huge as gumballs.

"The crowd went wild. They stood and clapped. Your grandfather removed his hat and took a bow, reveling in his greatest illusion of all time. It was a masterpiece! He had done it!" Tom Flaky clapped his hands together.

Molly jerked backward.

There was a glimmer in his eye.

"How did he do it?" asked Noah.

"He was an illusionist. So nobody really knew. Of course, the mayor had agreed to participate in the illusion, knowing that the publicity could only help his city." Tom Flaky clasped his hands together, and his voice grew cold. "But, then came the scream when the cabinet door opened."

"A scream? What happened?" Molly asked, clenching her fists like she'd heard the scream, herself.

Tom Flaky lowered his head, along with his voice. "Lying on the floor in a pool of blood was the mayor."

Molly gulped.

"DEAD."

"What happened?"

"A knife. Stabbed in the back."

"No," Molly said, not wanting to believe it.

Tom Flaky nodded his head. "Yes."

"Who did it?" asked Noah.

"The authorities blamed your grandfather. Just like that. No investigation, just a quick shotgun trial with a string of false witnesses. He was found guilty in less than an hour."

"No," Molly repeated softly, not understanding how somebody could be found guilty if they weren't really *guilty*. Especially her grandfather.

"It was a setup, the mob likely involved. But your grandfather was just a poor magician with little education and limited understanding of his rights."

"That's not fair!" Molly protested, not quite sure who she was mad at, but already starting to feel the loss of a grandfather she never knew. That her mother never knew.

Something wet stung at Molly's eye, and she quickly wiped it away.

"I'm sorry," said Tom Flaky, resting a hand on her shoulder.

"Me too." Molly couldn't look up. Noah was silent beside her.

Tom leaned forward "Now, here's the part where you come in," he said, placing a hand on Molly's knee.

CHAPTER 26

Swimming in Ocean Blue Eyes

His voice jolted Molly awake. For a second, she'd forgotten all about the Night Train and the Midnight Carnival and this spinning Ferris wheel. All she could think about was magic and blood and disappearing objects.

And unfairness.

Wasn't the world supposed to be fair?

"Your mom found her father a few years ago—well, *he* found *her*. But she had to keep it a secret, even from you."

"But, why?" Molly asked, not liking the sound of her mother keeping secrets from her, especially secrets about her grandfather.

"Because, people were looking for him. And he didn't want to risk being taken away again, not when he'd finally found his family. He just couldn't take the risk."

Molly couldn't believe her mother had kept something so big from her.

"They had a plan, though."

"What kind of plan?" Molly asked, looking out over the Carnival, at the black and gold tops of the tents down below.

"A plan to tell you the truth. A plan for one giant, fantastic, elaborate surprise to make up for all the years your grandfather had been gone— as well as to keep a final promise made by your mother. And, while they planned and saved up for the surprise, your grandfather stuck around in the meantime to be near you.

Molly's breath caught. "You mean he's *here?*"

"On Blue Rock Island?" asked Noah.

"Yes, indeed. He's been here for the last two years, keeping an eye on you the whole time."

"WHAT? How come I never saw him?"

"Because he was good at watching and not being seen."

"But, shouldn't I have noticed somebody watching me?" Molly thought of the old-fashioned blue car she'd noticed earlier today, wondering if that was what Tom Flaky was talking about. Even as she thought it, though, she didn't like the idea of somebody spying on her, especially her grandfather. That just felt too creepy. "He hasn't been *spying* on me, has he?"

"No. It wasn't in a way you'd think, Molly. Your grandfather didn't spy on you. But he did do everything he could to be around you. He wanted to be a part of your life, even if you couldn't know it was him just yet."

"How is that possible?" Molly asked, raising her voice.

"He wore disguises...some days the farmer at the fruit stand, and on others he delivered flowers. He also sold Christmas trees and was a carnival worker at Halloween," he said, his eyes shifting sideways to the string of lights surrounding them.

Molly's mouth dropped. She turned to Noah. His mouth hung open just as wide.

"But, he grew tired of all the disguises, and decided to stick to just one. He also had a thing for doughnuts."

The Ferris wheel seemed to be slowing, but Molly didn't notice as she tried to picture all the different faces in her head. That's when she realized her grandfather had been everywhere.

"And then your mother got sick," Tom Flaky said, bringing Molly's gaze away from Noah and back to the ocean blue eyes of Tom Flaky.

Yes, she did.

"And those people looking for your grandfather, they were getting closer to finding him—much *too* close. He couldn't go back to prison again. Not after having spent a lifetime there."

Molly was listening, but she was also watching, noticing details in his face she hadn't noticed before. Those eyes...the same eyes as her mother.

"I ran out of time, Molly," Tom Flaky said, not even realizing that he'd changed from talking in the third person to first. He was now talking about himself, and Molly took notice. "And your mother ran out of time, too."

Molly felt immovable, like her whole body had been changed to stone right here in the Ferris wheel car. She could feel Noah's hand on her arm; she could taste the salty breeze in her mouth. But nothing was as vivid and tangible as the truth she'd just uncovered right here in car number 3.

*Come fly with me in car number 3...*Tom Flaky was Molly's grandfather.

Molly knew he was still speaking to her, but she couldn't hear his voice anymore. And for some reason, she couldn't look him in the eye.

He cleared his throat, jolting her to attention. "Now, for the box," he said.

The box. Molly nodded. But she felt like she was in a bubble now, just floating around in the air as it carried her wherever it desired. "What about it?" she asked.

He leaned in close and lowered his voice. "I wanted to tell you who I was for so many years. But, I knew if I did that I couldn't be close to you anymore. Do you understand?"

Molly nodded, still staring at the box in her lap, though she felt numb.

"Now my fate is in your hands, Molly," he said, lifting her chin so that their eyes finally met.

It was?

His eyes were swirling blue like pools of water, sunken deep into his tanned, creviced face. They knew how to make Molly smile.

He added, "The power switch for the Ferris wheel is the blue button in the controller booth. Okay?"

"Okay," she said, having no idea what he was talking about. She was still floating around in that bubble, and no matter how fast she moved her arms or legs, she could only go where the bubble carried her.

"But, it's still your choice," Tom Flaky said, pulling Molly into a tight hug. At first she resisted, confused by what he was saying, taken aback by his sudden show of emotion. But there was something there, something inside that hug that made her feel safe and loved and understood, like her mom was in those arms. Trying to keep her promise.

Except, why did Molly feel like she was about to lose something else?

"Thank you for the last few years," Tom Flaky said, his voice cracking. Molly found his eyes again, trying to understand just what was happening. "I made the doughnuts just for you, Miss Molly. You will always be my very best customer."

Why did it sound like this was goodbye? Like he was going somewhere?

"Tom..." Molly started to say as he released her from his arms.

"Oh, and one last thing," he said, locking eyes with hers. "Make sure you follow the fireflies."

Follow the fireflies? What did that even mean?

She looked at Noah, hoping for some understanding. But his eyes were still fixed on Tom Flaky, who seemed about ready to do something.

Something BIG.

"And, now," said Tom Flaky as he stood up to face the other cars, his voice much louder than before, like an announcement to the whole world.

The music stopped as Tom's voice echoed through the air. He lifted the metal chest from off Molly's lap and held it up for Ruby and Wolfe and everyone else to see. The passengers in the other cars leaned over the edge of their cars, too, waiting, listening.

"For my final act! Inside this chest is proof of my true identity."

"What's he doing?" asked Noah as their car slowly pulled into position at the very bottom of the rotation, right in line with the wooden platform.

The Ferris wheel stopped.

"Molly…" Tom Flaky turned to her one more time, those eyes even more familiar than ever before. "I am set to leave the country tonight, in just under an hour." His voice cracked, there was moisture lining the edges of his eyes. "So, this, I'm afraid…is our final goodbye if that is what you choose."

Choose? Choose what? "I don't understand…" Molly looked to Noah for help, but he just shook his head and lowered his eyes. Molly could feel it building up inside her eyes, too.

"I have my passport and enough money…everything's in order and ready to go," he said.

"Go where? What are you talking about?"

Tom Flaky lowered his head. "It's time for you to know who I really am."

Molly swallowed hard, waiting for the words to be spoken out loud, though she already knew the truth.

He gazed directly up and across two cars behind them. Ruby and Wolfe waited. "Your mother, Olivia, was my daughter, which means that you are my—"

But he couldn't get the final word out, because Officer Wolfe and Ruby had jumped down from their car and landed on the platform beside car number 3. At the same time, they yelled the same command. "FBI! Freeze!"

The Ferris wheel erupted with screams.

Noah jumped backward.

Tom Flaky jerked his head toward Ruby and Wolfe, and lifted his hands in surrender as they flashed their badges and stepped toward him, pointing their guns in his face.

Molly stood beside Tom Flaky in the car, stunned. She dipped forward a bit, a wave of dizzy encircling her. Noah gently eased her into the bench. She couldn't seem to get enough air.

Officer Wolfe and Ruby Dodd unlocked the car door and pulled Tom Flaky toward them onto the platform. Molly lurched forward. She wanted to stop them, and was about to demand they let go of him, until she caught a subtle but noticeable look from Tom Flaky that stopped her. On his face was a sheet of calm, and very briefly, almost imperceptibly, he nodded his head, and smiled.

Molly froze, caught off guard.

And then she stepped backward and let Officer Wolfe put a gun to her grandfather's back.

CHAPTER
27

Act Two

Ruby slid her gun into her belt and did all the talking, telling Noah and Molly to stay put and not to do anything stupid.

"Give me the box," she demanded, holding open her hand.

"What box?" Molly asked, trying to play dumb.

"Look. I understand you're in a tough spot here, little girl."

"I'm not a little girl."

"I see. I am a Federal agent for the United States Government. Your grandfather is a convicted felon."

Molly gulped at such a pronouncement, and tried to meet Tom's gaze, but he wouldn't look her way. All she could think of at that moment were the words "convicted felon." They were such ugly words.

"Whatever is in his possession is property of the United States Government."

"No, it's not," Noah hesitantly stepped forward, almost as if he'd surprised himself by speaking up. When he realized he had everybody's attention, he continued, his voice stronger as he looked directly into Ruby's eyes. "You have no proof the box was ever his. For all you know, Molly found it in the dirt."

"That's a lie."

"Prove it." Noah folded his arms.

Ruby looked uncomfortable. "How about this? You can keep the box, as long as I get a good look at what's inside, first," she said.

Unsure what to do, Molly looked to Tom for help. He nodded his head just a smidge. Molly picked up the metal box and placed it on the platform, then stepped backward, and waited.

The platform creaked as Ruby drew closer.

Tom Flaky stepped forward. "How about putting the gun away. Just for now," he said, nodding his head in Molly and Noah's direction.

Ruby and Wolfe exchanged a look. When they seemed in agreement, Officer Wolfe holstered his gun back at his hip.

Tom gave Molly a little wink with his left eye as she stepped out of the car and onto the platform. Noah and Ruby and Wolfe leaned in closer as Ruby knelt to open the box. Aged wood and rusty metal creaked above them as passengers stranded in their suspended Ferris wheel cars leaned forward, everybody anticipating the contents inside the box.

Molly's eyes found Tom's. He stood at the top of the platform bathed in Ferris wheel lights behind everybody else, waiting for whatever was about to happen.

The bubble Molly had been floating in popped when she realized all at once just what he'd been telling her about the *blue power button at the controller booth.*

Her gaze shifted from Tom to the controller booth. It was only a few steps away. Her heart bellowed inside her at this choice her new grandfather had given her. To help him escape by turning out the lights and never seeing him again...or letting him be caught to keep him from leaving her again...

Molly didn't want to make that decision.

No. It *shouldn't* be up to her. Not something this big.

The lid was rusty, and resisted Ruby's effort to lift it. But she continued lifting until it stood up straight, the box wide open as everybody peered inside.

Molly fought the argument in her head as she lifted her eyes to find Tom again. *Her grandfather.* He lowered his eyes, as if letting her make the decision without his influence. She *knew* what she wanted. She *wanted* her long-lost grandpa to stay. How could she let him go when she just found him? At least if he was in jail…at least she could come visit him…

But that didn't feel right, as much as Molly wanted it to.

She nudged her way into the circle, trying to see for herself what great mystery lay inside the box. Sand filled the entire box, and on the very top of the sand pile was a crème-colored envelope, exactly like the one found in Molly's mailbox this morning. Printed in black across the front of the envelope was a name. Instead of Molly's name, however, was another name printed clearly across the front: **RUBY DODD.**

Molly's heart dipped as she stepped away from the box, away from the frenzy of Ruby and Wolfe and Noah and the crème-colored envelope.

Tom watched her, his face unreadable, but the edges of his mouth turned upward just like her mother's mouth. Molly looked more closely, more intently, trying to find more of her mother in her grandfather.

But it was too dark.

Could she do it? Could she really let Tom Flaky disappear just like her mother had? Molly's heart ached. She squeezed her hands into fists and slowly moved toward the controller booth, even though she wanted to remain standing exactly where she was.

Ruby snatched the envelope up in her hands, slid her finger under the flap and ripped it open. Everyone waited for her to read the message out loud.

Molly slipped inside the controller booth. It wasn't hard to find the correct button—there were only two buttons there: red and blue. And a red lever.

That was it.

Molly looked up, her hand hovering above the blue button.

Tom turned his head. She looked into his ocean blue eyes one last time, and then…

Pop!

Everything went dark. Screams echoed from passengers still suspended in the air, the metal creaking even louder. Molly dashed away from the controller booth, groping through the dark.

"Find the lights!" yelled Ruby. "The lights!"

Molly heard the scuffle of feet all around her.

Somebody knocked her to the ground, the sting of pain striking through her knee. She squealed in pain.

"Molly," Noah's voice called behind her. "Are you okay?"

All at once the lights popped on. Molly looked up to find Noah beside her. Ruby stood a few feet away, turning in circles. "Where is he?" she screamed, her eyes bulging.

"He's gone!" said Officer Wolf from inside the controller booth.

Ruby dropped the crème-colored envelope to the ground and reached for her gun, aiming it up and down and all around her.

Noah helped Molly to her feet and stood in front of her, as if to protect her. Officer Wolfe followed Ruby away from the Ferris wheel lights, into the shadows. They were frantic, both running around in circles, each taking a different side of the walkway.

Molly's gaze dropped to her feet, to the letter from Ruby's crème-colored envelope. It lay on the ground, only a few inches away.

She looked around her.

Noah had taken it upon himself to attend to the remaining passengers by sliding the red lever back and forth until each car found its way down to the platform.

Molly picked up the letter. Ruby's personal message from Tom Flaky read: **ACT 2: THE DISAPPEARING MAN.**

The disappearing man?

More like the *invisible* man. Molly still didn't know how it was possible to have run into her grandfather over and over again for the past two years without ever knowing who he really was. No clue. Nada! Shouldn't she have at least sensed something *familiar* about him? About everybody he'd pretended to be? She supposed he was a magician, but *still.*

After the last Ferris wheel car had stopped and unloaded, Noah found his place beside Molly, took the letter from her hand, and read through it. "Tom knew about the FBI the whole time," he said with much more enthusiasm than Molly felt, herself. "He planned the whole thing!" Noah seemed way too excited about the turn of events.

Sure, letting Tom escape had been her choice, and deep down she knew she had done the right thing—but she didn't know what to think about him leaving her so soon after finding her.

Something hurt inside her heart.

Ruby and Wolfe climbed back up the hill toward Molly and Noah, finally stopping at the base of the Ferris wheel platform, both out of breath. Ruby gaped at Molly. "Where did he go?"

Molly couldn't even look at her, and instead focused on her feet. "I just barely found out I had a grandpa. You really think I somehow know all his plans?"

Ruby kicked her foot against the bottom step.

"What else is in the box?" Wolfe asked Noah, like Noah was suddenly the box expert. Noah shrugged his shoulders, too bothered to even respond. Molly liked his new attitude.

Officer Wolfe looked to Ruby for approval, and then put the sole of his shoe to the side of the box to tip it over. Sand spilled across the platform, and the box tumbled down the steps and clanked against the ground.

But that was all that was inside. Just sand.

"Five years!" screamed Ruby, throwing her arms up into the air. "Gone. Just like that!"

"We'll find him again," Officer Wolfe said calmly.

"No. We won't. Our cover is blown!" Ruby yelled. She groaned and stormed down the hill, Officer Wolfe right behind her, their voices fading with the last of their footsteps until they finally disappeared into the shadows.

Molly sunk to the ground, wondering if she would ever feel right again.

CHAPTER

28

Gravity

When the last of the passengers had deserted the now lonely hill and returned to the gold and black tents at the bottom of the hill, Molly and Noah looked down over the Carnival. It seemed about finished now, but Molly wasn't ready for her adventure to end.

Not yet. Not like this.

She sighed and dropped her head, afraid to move. Noah gazed up at the empty Ferris wheel still lit but stalled, and like a burst of firecracker suddenly igniting the dark sky, came up with the perfect idea.

At first, Molly resisted when he grabbed her hand and led her toward an empty car. "What are you doing?" she protested.

But, Noah wouldn't give in. "I think we still have a little time left," he said, smiling. "And, I'm an expert with the big red lever now. So, have a seat, Miss Molly, and get ready for your very own Ferris wheel ride."

Molly's heart brightened despite its desire to deflate, and she lowered herself into the empty bench, waiting.

"You ready?" Noah yelled from where he stood next to the red lever.

Molly nodded.

Noah studied the control panel for a second, first finding the knob for the music, and then for the automatic rotation. After turning up the music to full blast, he pounded on the red button and leapt for Molly's car before it creaked forward and started to lift. The wind caught Molly's hair the higher they climbed, and Noah took a seat on the bench across from her.

Molly turned outward to view the grounds below them and the distant shoreline off in the distance. Everything felt so peaceful up here in this little tipsy car without any interruptions, especially compared to the chaos of noise and confusion she'd left down there. For a second, Molly watched Noah as he turned the other way. She studied the detail in his square jaw and short, dark hair, and at that moment Molly was grateful, most of all, for Noah in her life. *He wasn't going anywhere...at least she believed so.*

"Look!" Noah stood, shaking the car and making Molly grip the bench even tighter. They had reached the top of the ride and now seemed suspended up there, like they were floating in space, the stars close enough to scoop up with their hands. Frank Sinatra was belting out *Come fly with me, let's fly...let's fly away...*

It seemed fitting for the moment.

Molly held onto the metal railing at the side of the car and slowly stood, careful not to rock the car any more than necessary. The scattered lights of the city and both bridges spanning the bay were out there, smiling up at them. Molly almost waved, but felt dumb. Instead, she held on tight and fell back into her seat.

Suddenly, the sky was booming in explosions of color. And, as Frank Sinatra's voice faded, fireworks ignited everywhere on either side of them.

Molly smiled. Noah cheered.

She closed her eyes for a second, trying to imagine the Fourth of July last summer, her mother by her side as they watched the sky erupt in celebration.

"Molly." Noah's voice interrupted. "Are you okay?"

He was beside her, his hand on her knee. Molly looked up just as a colorful burst of red and gold set fire to the sky. Their car had almost reached the bottom of the rotation, making Molly wonder how long an uninterrupted Ferris wheel ride lasted.

Noah's hand was gone now, and he leaned back against the wooden seat, spreading both arms wide. He smiled. She smiled back.

"Did you have any idea Tom Flaky was related to you?" Noah asked. "Like, ever?"

"No. Not a clue. Makes me feel kind of dumb, though. Like, shouldn't I have noticed something? *Anything?*"

"Did your Mom ever say anything about him?"

"Only that he died when she was ten. That's it."

Noah looked the other way, out across the bay. They were almost to the top again. Molly liked the rotation, how the wheel kept returning back to the beginning, like a fresh start. It seemed the opposite of what happened in reality, the opposite of gravity—yet here they were, defying gravity, anyway.

A soft breeze lifted her hair. Goosebumps spread up and down her arms and legs.

"I'm sorry," Noah said.

Molly wanted to look away from him, embarrassed at his being so serious. But she also loved the way he watched her. It made her feel safe. And happy.

"It's okay. I just don't know what to do next. That's all."

But it was even more than that. Noah didn't know she was the one who turned off the lights. He didn't know that Molly had helped Tom escape...and she didn't think she could admit it, either. Not to him, not to anybody. Because she had been given one chance, not to let her grandfather leave. And she gave it up.

She just, for some reason, felt worse about forcing her grandfather to stay if he really didn't want to.

And he didn't, did he? Or he would have stayed.

With her.

The Ferris wheel started to slow just as the fireworks exploded in five different spots of white all at once. Molly and Noah remained in their seats, watching what seemed to be the grand finale. When the show ended, they unlatched the door and let themselves out.

From where they stood, they could see a crowd of train passengers already migrating toward the carnival entrance as the black and gold tents started to collapse one by one and the performers began gathering their things together.

The night of magic was coming to an end.

"You ready?" Noah asked, descending the steps.

Molly didn't want to go, but it was time, and she was tired.

"You kids had better hurry up. Don' want to miss the train," said a voice from the shadows.

Molly turned to find the shady outline of the whiskered, hunched-over firefly man standing by the control booth. With a *poof,* the blaring white lights illuminating the perimeter of the Ferris wheel went out.

Molly shivered.

"Oops. Looks like you need some light," said the man, lifting up a jar of fireflies and handing it to Molly.

Her heart stopped. She held the wire handle tightly in her fingers. "Thank you!" she exclaimed, beaming with joy. Molly couldn't believe it—after all this…at least she would have her own firefly jar.

They could hear the train's engine rumbling, like it was ready to take off.

Molly and Noah ambled down the pathway, but stopped when the firefly man cleared his throat to relay one last thing. "It's dark out there. Better follow the fireflies."

Molly spun around at the familiar phrase. "What did you say?" she asked, remembering that same phrase spoken to her by Tom Flaky only a half hour ago.

But they were met only with silence, and it was much too dark to see an old firefly man hiding in the shadows.

"What's going on?" Molly whispered to Noah.

Whooo-hoooooooo! The train whistled again.

"I don't know. But, it sounds like we'd better hurry."

They started down the hill, but stopped again at the sound of a deeper, more familiar voice following them from behind. "They'd always be watching, Molly. That's why I have to disappear. When it's safe again, I'll come back to you."

Molly whirled around, searching the seeping blackness for that familiar face hiding somewhere in the night, but she couldn't see past the glowing light coming from her firefly jar.

"Come on," said Noah, tugging at Molly's hand.

Whooo-hooooooooo!

"That's three times now. You'd better go," said Tom Flaky.

With Molly's hand clasped in his, Noah sprinted toward the train as the last of the passengers boarded. Molly clutched her firefly jar as they tried to blend into the crowd while she fought the smile pushing through her frown.

CHAPTER 29

The long-haired man watched Molly and Noah board the train. Once he was satisfied they were safely aboard and the FBI agents out of sight, he removed his wig and sunglasses, changed out of his hippie clothes, and stuffed everything into a bag.

Careful to steer clear of Molly, he climbed aboard just as the train pulled away from the station. He then slunk in an empty seat in the very back of car number one, and thought of Olivia.

How he missed her.

CHAPTER 30

The Ghosts of Bell's Bluff

They were one of the last passengers to board. Noah treaded through the aisle ahead of Molly, his hands running along the tops of the benches.

Molly followed close behind Noah while observing the other passengers. Some were already asleep in their seats. While many eyes were still bright, others seemed a little droopy. Molly felt like hers were somewhere in between. Br*oopy*.

"Ladies and Gentlemen, please find your seat. The Night Train will be leaving in approximately two minutes. We hope you have enjoyed your exclusive Midnight Carnival experience at Bell's Bluff. The final leg of your adventure takes us into

the never-before-seen dungeons of Bell's Bluff Prison.

"Did you hear that?" Molly asked Noah, not sure if she really wanted to participate in this part of the tour. "Is this part really necessary?"

"Are you kidding?" asked Noah, sitting safely inside the train in his assigned row. "Seeing the inside of a prison is going to be the best part of the whole night!"

Molly tucked her firefly jar beneath the bench where it wouldn't get knocked over, and leaned back in her seat. "I thought the Night Train was supposed to be fun. Old prisons are *not* fun."

"Relax," he said, scooting closer to Molly. "I'll keep you safe."

She pushed him away.

The little lights on the floor lit up, and once again as the train started forward, a cloud of smoky, purple mist rose up from the floor. They swayed sideways as the train pitched to the right and entered into a tunnel, leaving behind the starry sky and any trace of light. The purple mist transitioned into green and then pink, finally settling on smoky white.

Molly peered out the window, but found only rocky cliff walls on either side of her. They picked up speed, and she clenched her fists and pressed the soles of her feet into the floor, hoping for the best. Outside the window, row after row of spooky, arched tunnels, zoomed by, each empty passage burrowing deeper into the cliffs.

The back of Molly's head pressed against the bench as the train started climbing upward before leveling out again, under the stars. Moonlight hit both sides of the car, throwing light across the back of each seat.

Molly jumped at the announcer's voice. *"Bell's Bluff was converted to a United States Federal Penitentiary in 1952.*

"I don't really care about this," Molly whispered to Noah, who motioned for her to be quiet.

"For over fifty years Bell's Bluff was most famous for having one of the best disciplined and most secure penal institutions in the entire country. That is, until 2008, when one of Bell's Bluff's inmates escaped."

"This is the part that gets interesting," said Noah, raising his eyebrows.

"But—"

"Shhhh!"

Fine.

The train slowed down as it passed through a building in ruins on the left and a graveyard specked with crosses and old tombstones on the right.

"Most assumed the inmate tried to swim to freedom, only to be dashed to pieces on the rocks at the bottom of the cliffs, or even eaten by sharks."

Sharks!

"After the escape, Bell's Bluff was closed permanently. Some say they can still hear the screams of inmates who died at Bell's Bluff echoing through the underground tunnels. And some say they hear the clanking of chains from the ghosts of Bell's Bluff who never left.

Can you?

Screeeeeeeech.

Clang!

Whooooooooooh.

Eerie noises crawled through the train like a thin string of fog. Molly shivered as a cold breeze whistled through the car, gently lifting the hair off her shoulders. This was definitely not her idea of fun, though Noah seemed to be enjoying himself just fine.

Lights flashed through the windows. She blinked against the bright flashes, and her eyelids felt heavy, like little weights trying to pull everything down. Molly continued to push back, to rub her eyes, hoping to stay awake so she wouldn't miss anything else…

Pop! Pop! Pop!

Molly drew in a quick breath and opened her eyes. The train cabin was alight with color.

Noah squeezed her arm. "Look!" he said.

Little bursts of color had ignited throughout the train, like mini fireworks going off, one after another. Molly held out her hand, trying to catch a bright pink blast. But it only tickled her skin and dissolved just as another purple burst exploded in its place.

Pop! Pop! Pop!

Color everywhere. Voices loud and soft through the train car.

And then, silence.

The last sparks of color had fizzled out, leaving everybody in the dark. Each passenger held still, waiting, wondering what was next.

The overhead lights turned on, and the train stopped.

The Night Train was over.

Passengers stood and pulled on their coats or picked up their purses and bags. Everyone looked as wasted as Molly felt. Feet were dragging, smiles had faded, and big, gaping yawns were spreading from face to face.

Molly collected her firefly jar and led the way down the aisle, Noah following right behind her. At the top of the step, she stopped and contemplated this underground train station again, hoping to keep it alive in her memory.

She scanned the thinning crowd. Some had souvenirs from the carnival, things like stuffed animals or bags of candy. Others held clear, tied-up bags of fish. But nobody, not one person had a firefly jar.

Just Molly.

That seemed a little strange, considering she'd seen at least ten or twelve jars hanging from the trees. Maybe nobody had been able to think of a perfect wish.

Somebody nudged Molly from behind, prompting Noah and Molly to continue on down the steps onto the platform.

"Which way is out?" she asked, feeling disoriented without a train official wearing fancy white gloves helping them every step of the way. Noah boldly started walking down the platform in one direction, obviously better at remembering directions and landmarks than Molly. But suddenly, he stopped.

"What's wr—" she started to ask, but stopped, too, when she saw who was waiting for them by the brick wall.

"Hello, Molly."

She felt all the color drain from her face.

Dad.

CHAPTER
31
Midnight Detour

For sure she was in trouble. She *had* to be in trouble.

But, if that were the case, then where were those frown lines carved like a river in between Dad's eyes? Why wasn't he already yelling at her?

"Hi," Molly squeaked from where she stood, still afraid to come any closer, especially with him standing there in his black police uniform.

"Hi, Molly. Hello, Noah." Dad nodded.

"Hello, Officer Pepper."

The echo of voices throughout the train station faded as the rest of the passengers exited through all different Night Train entrances scattered throughout the island.

Molly's dad put his hand on her shoulder. It was gentle. "Molls, I think you have a lot to tell me about tonight—"

"I know. I don't even know where to start, but—"

"I have a lot to tell you, too."

"You do?" she asked, confused.

"Yes, but what do you say we first find our way out of here and get Noah back home so his parents will stop worrying?"

Oh, shoot, Molly thought. *Noah's parents were in the know?*

Noah lowered his head while slowly shaking it back and forth. Molly could already see the earlier boost of confidence starting to fade. She thought of his goal number three. His determination to beat his fears, and wondered what his Dad and the kids at school would really think of him if they knew how brave he'd been tonight.

But, Molly guessed it wasn't up to her or even up to them to prove Noah was brave. She supposed it was really up to Noah to believe it was true.

They followed Officer Pepper up through the opening in the brick wall, and stepped into the circular elevator. Somehow he knew which button to push. The elevator lifted them up...up...until it had stopped and the three of them were exiting through the door, down the hidden hallway and back up the stairs.

None of them spoke as they climbed the wooden staircase up through the trapdoor marked number 8, and on down the grassy hill to where Officer Pepper's cruiser was parked at the curb at the top of Candlestick Hill.

They dropped Noah off at his house. His Mom answered the door with a hug—which also surprised Molly. Sure, she was normally a friendly lady, but at midnight?

"Dad," Molly started to say when she noticed a strange car sitting in their driveway. She was certain it had the same familiar shape as the old-fashioned blue car that had been following her all day.

"Yes?" he said, backing the car out into the street, mysteriously driving past their house.

"Wait...where are we going?"

"Just for a drive."

"Why aren't we going home?"

"Because it looked to me like we had visitors at home, and I'm not in the mood for visitors. Are you?"

Molly shook her head and clutched her firefly jar to her chest, feeling herself becoming lost in the little flashes of light shining in through the windshield. Out her window she could see the calm, dark surface of the bay, making her realize they were driving along Perimeter Drive, the two-lane road that encircled the island.

"Tell me about your day," her dad said.

Molly knew he wasn't asking for boring details to keep up conversation. He knew where Molly had been tonight, and this was his request for the truth. After an entire day of secrets, she was ready to tell him.

Molly placed her jar of fireflies on the seat between them, and leaned into his side as she told him everything...starting with the Night Train invitation, and the clues and the key, to the suspicious blue car...to Officer Wolfe...

"You are very observant," he said at one point, like he was proud.

His smile told her to keep going.

So, Molly kept going...

His eyes grew big at the mention of the lights and colored fog and acrobats on the train; he laughed out loud at how much food she and Noah had eaten; he smiled when she told him all about the Midnight Carnival with all its noise, the delicious food, the black and gold booths...and the firefly jars...

It was a huge relief for Molly to tell him everything, like she had placed all her worries inside a paper bag, and then handed the bag over to her dad for safekeeping.

When Molly came to the part about Tom Flaky in disguise, who happened—just happened to be her grandpa, she paused and gazed up into her dad's eyes when he turned his head away from the road for a second.

For some reason, he seemed *not* to be surprised.

"Did you know he was my grandpa?" Molly asked.

Mr. Pepper drew in a deep breath, and then told her about meeting her grandpa for the first time last year…just before Molly's mother died. He then told Molly about *his* night, starting with the grocery sack he'd found in the front seat of his cruiser.

"What was inside?" Molly asked.

Randy Pepper wasn't ready to tell her just yet. First, he had something to show her. He brought the car to a stop at the side of the road, and then turned on the interior light.

"Why are we stopping here?" Molly asked, glancing out the window to the lookout point where tourists liked to stop for pictures. Though tonight, only the light of the moon met them here.

He pulled from the backseat a rolled-up

poster, and placed it right in Molly's lap. Molly unrolled it. "What are you doing with Tom's poster?" she asked, realizing she was staring at the old black and white poster she'd seen earlier today in Tom Flaky's doughnut shop.

"Just look at it," he insisted, pointing to one particular photo at the bottom.

Molly did as she was told, focusing on the photo of the surly-looking convict with a pair of deep-set eyes hidden under thick eyebrows. No matter how she stared, she still felt like she was missing something. All she saw was a scary-looking prisoner—whose face was probably now going to give her nightmares tonight.

"I don't see anything, Dad. Just a mug shot of a murderer."

Randy's hand fell on her shoulder. "Are you sure about that? Keep looking. There's more."

"There is?"

Molly searched for more details. Her gaze fell on the black plaque hanging around the convict's neck, with small, white numbers marking him as a prisoner. BB1331.

That number seemed so familiar…

Beneath his photo a small paragraph further described the mysterious prisoner. She leaned in closer, reading the description out loud.

Tom Moody (born September 1, 1950 – missing since June 13, 2008) was a Bell's Bluff inmate who escaped from the island in June 2008 and was never seen again. Born in Chicago, IL, he was convicted of first-degree murder, his first and only known crime at age 34. He was said to have an IQ of 133.

"He sure had a thing for the number 13, don't you think?"

"Ah…you noticed."

"It's pretty obvious, once you start reading about him. I wonder if back then the number 13 was as unlucky as it is now."

"Hard to say."

"How do you think he really escaped? Or did he get eaten by sharks like everyone says?"

Randy Pepper remained silent. So, she kept reading.

On January 3, 1985, Moody was shipped from Chicago to Bell's Bluff Federal Penitentiary, where he was prisoner #BB1331 for 13 years. According to accounts from

other inmates, he began devising
his escape within a year of his
arrival at Bell's Bluff.

BB1331.

Why did that number look and sound so
familiar?

Tom Moody.

Molly remembered hearing Ruby call the
Ferris wheel operator *Moody.*

Wait a second...

Her head was suddenly spinning. She looked
up at her dad, afraid to speak.

"*Dad...*" she started to say, but was too
shocked at this revelation to know how to finish
her sentence. She re-read the paragraph, and this
time the number 13 jumped out all over the
place. She thought of today's date: June 13th.

"*This* is Tom Flaky?" she asked, pointing to
the mug shot of the escaped convict named Tom
Moody. "My *grandfather?*" It couldn't be.

"Yes," Randy said.

Molly closed her eyes, remembering a few
hours ago in the brick hallway under Candlestick
Hill, staring at the number 13 etched into the
wood at the top of the door.

Number 13.

And the train. THE TRAIN!

She could picture it in her head this very

moment—sparkling in shiny gold and black paint, the number 1331 painted in gold.

1331

What other clues out there had she overlooked? Tom Moody had been out tonight in plain sight for Molly and the whole world to see, and even the FBI missed it.

Molly felt her mouth turn up at the corners, at least briefly. She had to laugh inside—Tom Moody, the escaped convict and once-famous magician...had brought everything together tonight for one final spectacular show. His best one yet.

The Ferris wheel
The train.
And the carnival. And the fireflies.

"How did he do it?" Molly asked, trying to put everything together in her head.

"How did he do *what?* Escape from prison?"

"Not just escape...how did he do *everything?* The whole idea? How did the FBI miss it?"

"The papers say he was a genius. A mastermind."

"But, why? Why did he do it? Why didn't he run far away when he had the chance? Why come back?"

"Well, that's an easy answer," Randy said, his lips curling upward at the corners of his mouth.

"It is?"

Randy nodded. "For you. He did it all for you, Molly."

Molly drew in a breath, deep and long. She didn't know what to say to that.

Randy started laughing, a soft, deep chuckle, as he shook his head and placed his hand on Molly's knee. "Can you believe it?"

Molly *couldn't* believe it. The Night Train, the Midnight Carnival, the clues and fireflies and the Ferris wheel—they had all been created for *her*.

For Molly.

"I don't know, Dad...I don't think he'd do everything just for me. It seems like there has to be more to it."

"Well, I suppose there is a little bit more to it."

"There is?"

"Yes. Your Mom."

"Mom? But, she's not even here to see it."

"Yes, but she was the one who promised to take you to catch fireflies and ride the Ferris wheel in Chicago, didn't she?"

Molly nodded her head.

"Until she got sick." Randy Pepper had the sniffles tonight.

Molly stared straight ahead, refusing to meet that solemn, glossy-eyed look she was always trying to avoid. She wanted that crinkled smile back, fast.

Randy continued. "Tom made a promise of his own—to help his daughter keep her promise to you. But, your Mom died before her promise was ready, Molls. She was supposed to be here, tonight, too. We were all supposed to be here, together," he said, choking out the last word.

Molly tried to fight her own glossy-eyed look, but didn't know how to keep it from coming. She tilted the firefly jar on its side, trying to focus on the little yellow lights floating around inside the jar while her dad found his voice again.

"When she was a little girl, she wanted her very own jar of fireflies, too, you know."

"She did?"

Randy nodded his head.

"Did she ever get one?" Molly asked.

"No...she couldn't think of her very best wish, either."

What? How did he know about that?

"Molly, what is your very best wish?"

"I don't know what you mean."

"If you could have any wish in the whole world, what would it be?"

Molly felt frustrated, and dropped the jar back into her lap. "But wishes aren't real. They don't really come true."

"That's not what I asked. It doesn't matter whether or not they come true. It just matters what your very best wish would be. What is it?"

Molly didn't even have to think. Because she knew the first moment the firefly man had asked her to make it, that she could never make her very best wish. Not then. Not now. She couldn't make a wish she knew was impossible to come true. She just couldn't.

Her dad didn't push it, and Molly was glad for that as he started up the car and started driving home.

"For a policeman, you seem to know a lot about fireflies," Molly said, lifting her eyebrows. "How do you even know about wishes and firefly jars?"

Randy turned the corner onto Penny Lane, and then looked in Molly's eyes. "Because, I was there."

"What do you mean you were there? *Where?*" she asked.

His face lit up and he cracked a little smile. "Everywhere you went tonight, I was there, too."

WHAT?

"I couldn't let you just sneak out of the house and wander around the top of Candlestick Hill all by yourself, now could I?"

"You…you *knew* about…about my letter…and Candlestick Hill…and the Night Train…and *everything?*" Molly asked, relieved when she noticed the strange car was no longer parked in their driveway.

Randy nodded, trying to hold in his laugh as he pulled into the driveway and shifted into park.

"Why didn't you tell me?"

"It was your adventure, Molls. Not mine. I had to respect that," he said, reaching over the seat and pulling into his lap a grocery sack.

"What's in the sack, Dad?" Molly wondered how much more peculiar her night could get.

Randy reached into the sack and pulled out a long-haired wig and a pair of sunglasses. "I wanted you to experience a little magic for a change," he said, holding the disguise up.

Molly couldn't believe it—her dad in disguise?

"It was you! On the train," Molly exclaimed, remembering the long-haired man dropping the clue that had led her to the Ferris wheel. "How come I didn't recognize you?" she asked, still finding it hard to believe her dad had been there with her the whole time…even when she thought she was alone.

Especially when she was alone.

"I'm pretty good at what I do," he winked.

She fingered the wig, unable to grasp the fact that her dad had been following her the entire night. "Where did you even get this?" she asked.

"Let's just say Tom knows a thing or two about disguises."

Molly thought back through the night, recalling a familiarity she'd seen in the eyes of more than one stranger—the tall, proper Englishman in the white gloves, the old, whiskery firefly man with the raspy voice *and* the Ferris wheel operator.

Could her grandfather have been all those people? Had she been surrounded by a bit of magic all night without even knowing it?

Molly felt a rush of happiness spilling out of her just like Officer Wolfe's cream-filled doughnut bursting at the seams, and she leaned across the seat, throwing her arms around her dad. "Thank you for letting me have my adventure," she said, adding, "and for helping Mom keep her promise."

The firefly jar tipped over and rolled onto the floor when she released her arms from Randy's neck. Randy rescued it from the floor, setting it back down on the seat, but not before Molly noticed some kind of writing on the base of the jar.

"Dad!" she said, lifting the jar up by its handle. "There's a message on the bottom!"

Sure enough, scribbled along the bottom of the jar in faint, black ink, was an address. 174 Candlestick Hill.

"Another clue!" Molly added.

But there was no time for celebration.

The screeching of rubber skidding to a stop and the flash of spinning lights surrounded their car, followed by a too-familiar voice demanding that they exit their car.

CHAPTER
32
Risky Business

"You've got to be kidding me," Randy said, glancing in his rearview mirror.

"Dad, what's going on?" Molly asked.

Randy sighed. "It looks like Officer Wolfe isn't done with us yet."

Molly whirled around, trying to see out the window. But the spinning of red and white made her dizzy. "What? NO! Dad. They'll take my firefly jar."

Randy sighed, holding onto Molly's hand. "I know, Molls. But, we don't really have a choice."

As Randy reached for the door handle, Molly's heart raced. She *couldn't* give in to Officer Wolfe—not now, not when she still held one more clue in her hands, one more clue that just might reveal a final hint about her grandfather.

Could she hide the jar? Molly quickly scanned the interior of the car, and then stopped, realizing that hiding the firefly jar wouldn't keep Officer Wolfe from returning to the mailbox before night's end. If he *knew* about it in the first place.

"Dad, wait," Molly said, pulling at his arm. "Officer Wolfe knows about Candlestick Hill, doesn't he?"

"Yes," he said. "He followed you up there tonight."

"And the mailbox?"

Randy thought for a minute. "If he followed you, then I'd say he knows about the mailbox, too."

Molly squeezed her dad's arm. "Then, he'll find whatever is inside the mailbox, won't he? Especially if he takes my firefly jar."

"I suppose so."

"But it's my last clue, Dad! I have to find it before he does."

"I understand, Molly. But we don't have very many options here," he said at the sound of the loudspeaker demanding again that Randy Pepper exit his vehicle.

No, thought Molly. There had to be another option. This. Was. Not. It.

Randy looked in her eyes. "I'm sorry, Molls. I don't have a choice."

Molly thought of everything she'd been through tonight—of the promise of adventure, to the reality of unfulfilled promises. She thought of the risk her grandfather took to fulfill them, of her father wearing a wig just to make sure she was safe, of Noah's unwavering determination to stick by her side even in the face of his own fears. That was when she realized that loving people meant taking risks. That love was a risk in and of itself because there was no guarantee anyone would make it out okay.

And, the bigger the risk, the greater the proof that love was ever there in the first place.

"Dad," she said, slinking low in the seat. "I have a plan."

"You do?" he said, listening.

And then, Randy Pepper took a risk, too. He opened the door and stepped out with his hands high in the air, and made his way toward the lights.

"Turn around," commanded the voice.

Randy did as he was told.

"Where's your daughter?"

Randy played dumb. "My daughter? Why, she's asleep, of course. Where else would she be at one o'clock in the morning?"

Molly could hear two other officers closing in around him. It made her sad to think of the tables turning on him like this. Still, with the firefly jar clutched in her hands, she quietly slid along the seat and poked her head out the door hanging wide open, waiting for the perfect moment.

The first thing she saw was the back of Officer Wolfe's head. He stood facing her dad while Ruby waited in a nearby car, talking on her phone.

Everybody was busy...

Except, it looked to Molly like two other officers were making their way up the walkway to the front door. Probably planning to check on Molly, to make sure Randy Pepper wasn't lying.

Molly *had* to move. *Now.* She didn't have a choice. There were no perfect moments. Not when you were risking everything.

She slid out the door and dropped onto the driveway, slinking along the cool cement until she was hidden behind her dad's cruiser.

When she heard the click of her front door unlocking and the swoosh of the door swinging inward, Molly turned and ran through the grass, across Noah's yard.

But she stopped cold at the dark figure standing in front of her.

CHAPTER
33

What a Friend Would Do for a

Friend…

"What are you doing here?" Molly asked Noah, pulling him with her into the bushes. He was still dressed in his head-to-toe black getup, however it seemed much more fitting now that they were on the run from the law.

"I heard all the commotion outside and wanted to see what was going on. Check it out—I climbed out my window this time," he said, with a big smile.

Molly wanted to congratulate him on his second act of rebellion, but knew it had to wait. "I'll explain later, but right now I have to get to the top of Candlestick Hill before Officer Wolfe figures out where I'm going," Molly said, darting across Noah's neighbor's lawn and out into the street.

Noah chased after her. "I'm coming with you."

"What about your parents?" Molly asked. "Aren't you worried they'll discover you sneaked out again?"

"A little. But I'm more worried about Officer Wolfe right now than them. He's a lot scarier."

At the bottom of the hill they stopped to catch their breath. A dog barked from behind a fence, making Molly jump. "Do you hear any sirens?" she asked, looking both ways.

"No. Not yet."

Most of the porch lights had been extinguished, leaving only the faint glow of the firefly jar guiding their way as they climbed the hill. This time of night was too quiet for Molly. She longed for the sound of the ferry whistle or an errant car horn traveling across the island. Even the seagulls, whose mocking calls she usually ignored, were high on her wish list this very moment.

Espccially when they heard the one sound they dreaded.

Sirens.

"Hurry," Molly said, though she knew Noah could run faster than her.

Only two houses to go…

Molly glanced behind her, down the hill. Red and white lights met at the bottom before smoothly charging up the hill.

They ran faster, willing their legs to push through the burn tearing through their muscles. Finally, they stopped in front of the mailbox and tore open the lid, the glow from the firefly jar lighting up the inside cavity, illuminating the edges of a rusted metal box sitting inside.

On top of the box was a crème-colored envelope with Molly's name printed in black ink on the front: Molly Pepper

First, she opened the envelope. A short note was scribbled inside.

> Inside this box are the only things they let me keep when I was sent to prison 27 years ago. It is the last thing left I have of my past. Now, it is yours, Molly. Take care of it.
>
> Love–
>
> Your Grandfather

Molly brought the box out of the mailbox and held it close to her, even though she knew Officer Wolfe would tear it from her hands as soon as he arrived.

She couldn't stand the thought.

Behind them, Molly felt the rumbling of police cars, the sound of her own hope being shattered. Now she would never have the chance to see what was inside the box—Tom's last possessions, her grandfather's final words.

"Here, give it to me!" yelled Noah, yanking everything from Molly's hands and dashing away into the empty lot behind the mailbox.

"What? Why?" she asked, confused by Noah's sudden demand.

But before he could explain, the screaming whirl of lights breached the hill, followed by two pairs of headlights—the whole circus of noise and lights and commotion coming to a halt directly in front of Molly.

Molly turned around, squeezing her eyes shut against the glare.

"Step away from the mailbox," said Officer Wolfe through his obnoxious loudspeaker.

Molly advanced blindly, the lights too bright for her to see where she was going. In an instant she felt the familiar presence of her dad at her side, pulling her into his arms.

"You okay, Molls?" he asked, kneeling in front of her.

She whispered yes in his ear, but wouldn't

let go of him. She needed his familiar, comfortable arms to hold her. It was the only place she felt safe right now.

"Did you find it?" he whispered.

"Yes," she said, even quieter, finally pulling back and finding his eyes. "Did you get into trouble, Dad?" she asked, placing her hands on his shoulders, touching her fingers to his cheeks.

"Yes and no. But you don't need to worry about it. Everything will work out fine." Molly wasn't sure if she could believe him. She'd heard that phrase before, and everything *did not* work out fine.

Suddenly, Ruby's loud, globe-like face had breached Molly's safe place. "Where is it?" she demanded, making Molly cringe.

"Where is *what?*" Molly asked, lingering at Randy's side.

"Whatever you came up here for. You obviously came here for a reason. Moody left you a message once before, so I'm guessing he's done it again."

"There isn't a message," answered Molly, turning her head the other way. She noticed Officer Wolfe pacing around the end of the cul-de-sac, and two other officers shining their flashlights along the sidewalk and off into the bushes.

Where was Noah?

"Tell me now, young lady, or I'll..."

"You'll what?" Molly spun around hard, making Ruby stumble backward into the curb. "He's gone, don't you see? And you don't even care! All you care about is capturing your prisoner. Well, he's the only thing I had left that's connected to my mom, and you ran him off!" Molly leapt forward at Ruby, pushing her back.

Randy pulled her away, into the circle of his arms where she collapsed in tears.

Officer Wolfe stopped pacing. The other officers stopped talking. The sound of Molly's quiet, muffled whimpers filled the air at the top of Candlestick Hill while Noah clutched the box even tighter to his chest and ducked further into the bushes.

Ruby straightened her jacket and cleared her throat. She then turned around and paced back to the police car, quietly slipping inside. The other officers followed suit, silently climbing into their cars, too.

That left only Officer Wolfe standing by himself at the end of the cul-de-sac, his flashlight still waving around the grassy field, still looking for something or someone lurking out there in the dark. This was his golden moment—proof for Ruby and the rest of the team that he knew what he was doing, that he was worthy of his position, that he could be trusted and deserved to be promoted...

Officer Wolfe took another step into the grassy field, certain now that he'd heard the crack of a branch, even a heavy intake of breath.

But, he stopped and turned, his eyes resting directly on Molly Pepper and her father. They lingered there, even as he heard another cracking twig behind him. First he lowered his eyes, and then his flashlight, as he came to the realization that some things in life mattered more than others. And then, slowly, Officer Wolfe treaded away through the tall grass and climbed back into his car.

When the spinning lights and the sound of engines had faded, Noah emerged from the bush. Randy Pepper pulled him into their hug. And then, with the light of the fireflies guiding their way, Randy and Molly and Noah walked home.

CHAPTER
34

The Curious Life of a Firefly

The sound of a lawnmower being pushed up and down Molly's front lawn was what probably pulled her out of sleep. She turned over, squeezing her eyes shut again after opening them seemed to take too much effort. After finally lifting them for good, she caught a glimpse of her clock atop her dresser, and congratulated herself for successfully sleeping in later than her dad for the first time in her life.

After kicking back her covers, she sat up to sunlight peeking in through the blinds, smiling at the hint of blue sky waiting for her instead of dingy fog. Molly found it surprising how easy it felt to smile this morning.

At the foot of her bed, almost touching the

tips of her pink-painted toes, Molly glimpsed at the box—*the* rusted metal box with dented corners and a metal latch that used to be hidden inside the mailbox at 174 Candlestick Hill.

Molly scooted forward until she was right beside it, suddenly realizing she hadn't opened it yet. When they'd reached the bottom of the hill, Noah had found his stashed bicycle and cruised the rest of the way home, but Molly had been too tired; she climbed onto her dad's back for a piggy-back ride and must have fallen asleep on the way home.

Now, she glanced around her room, as if somebody was standing over her shoulder or hiding in the closet, watching her. It seemed that lately somebody was always watching her.

But, right now she was alone, so she opened the lid.

Inside were old photos with rounded corners. She handled them carefully. They were faded and yellowed in spots, each one capturing different people—a redheaded girl in pigtails and freckles, a man with thick, dark hair wearing a tall black hat, and a gold and black striped vest...*a magician doing tricks*...

The red-haired girl clapped her hands in one photo. In another she mugged for the camera with a big, gap-toothed smile. The dark-haired man with the mustache had been captured in the act of throwing the girl high in the air so it looked like she was floating.

Like a magic trick.

Molly flipped to the next photo and stopped.

A shiny, clear Mason jar rested at the very edge of a table, lit up inside by little glowing fireflies. Just behind the jar in the darkened background was a hazy face of a girl resting her chin on the table. Her brown eyes were bright and wide as she stared at the jar of fireflies. Molly turned the photo over. Printed in blue ink was a name and date: *Olivia, 1985.* The year Tom went to prison.

She placed the pile of photos on the bed and dug further into the box, looking for more treasures.

The lawnmower stopped, making Molly wonder if Dad had finished up and would be coming to wake her soon. She hurried.

There were only two more things inside the box—a wrinkled-up brown paper sack, and a crème-colored envelope addressed to Molly. It looked identical to the one she'd found inside her mailbox yesterday.

First, she opened the crumpled sack and screamed. A thick wad of one-dollar bills—no, *one hundred* dollar bills!—were tucked inside and tightly rolled into a giant spiral bigger than Molly's fist. She could not believe her eyes. Never in her life had she seen that much money. Not even on TV!

Molly loved how the wad of cash felt in her hand, and reluctantly set it aside to open the crème-colored envelope. But after reading the message, she felt more confused than ever:

Firefly Facts:

1. Fireflies can only live in a warm, humid environment (or a pseudo-environment created for them inside a jar).

HOWEVER,

2. Fireflies can only live in a jar for a few days.

Have you wished your impossible wish yet?

That was it? A riddle about fireflies?

Molly checked the backside of the letter, just in case she'd missed something. But it was blank.

"Molls."

Molly jumped. Her dad was standing in her

doorway. He'd brought with him the outdoorsy aroma of cut grass and motor oil.

"You scared me!" she yelled.

"I see you've looked through the box," he said, finding an empty place to sit on Molly's bed.

She nodded.

He shuffled through the photos. "I went through it last night, after tucking you in," he admitted.

"You did?" Molly felt a little let down, like he'd raided her treasure.

"Yes."

"Do you know what this note means?" Molly showed him the paper, but he didn't pick it up. "Why did Tom Flaky give me another riddle? About fireflies, this time."

"I think you can figure it out. You've figured everything else out so far."

"But that was with Noah's help!"

"Then maybe you should ask for Noah's help again," he said, chuckling.

Why was he talking in riddles, now, too? All Molly wanted anymore was a simple, straight answer. No more riddles.

"That sure is a lot of money," Randy Pepper said, eyeing the wad of bills on the bed.

"How much do you think it is?"

"Well...I already counted it," he said with a

straight face and serious eyes.

"You did?"

"Yes." He let loose a slight smile.

"And?"

"And..."

Molly punched her dad in the arm. "Come on, Dad! You're killing me. How much is it?"

"Eight-thousand dollars."

"WHAT?" Molly bounded up to her knees. "Where did he get it all?"

Dad patted Molly's knee. "I asked him the same question last night when he told me about how he'd created the Night Train."

"What did he say?"

"Believe it or not, Tom made quite a few friends when he was in prison."

That made perfect sense to Molly. "Everyone likes a magician," she said.

"Apparently. One of those friends had buried his life savings years ago, and told Tom the money was his to keep if he ever escaped from Bell's Bluff."

"Wow. That's a big promise."

"Not to a prisoner. I think the promise of freedom, even for a friend, would be worth more than a treasure you could never have."

Molly thought about that. It brought to mind her mother, for some reason, though she wasn't particularly sure why.

"What does Tom...I mean, *my grandpa* want *me* to do with all this money?" she asked, feeling funny about taking something so valuable from somebody she knew very little about. "Eight-thousand dollars is a lot of money for a kid."

"You don't have to decide this second. But I do think we need to come up with a good hiding place for it, at least until things blow over a little.

A hiding place. Molly wondered where in the world they could hide eight thousand dollars without anybody noticing.

There was a soft tapping on Molly's door, and in walked Noah. Molly shoved everything back inside the rusted metal box and closed the lid.

"Hello, Noah," Randy said, shaking Noah's hand like they were two gentlemen.

"Hi, Officer Pepper."

"I hope your parents weren't too upset about last night."

"No, I think they were okay," Noah said, his eyes shifting sideways.

"They didn't mind you helping me with that emergency last night, did they?" Randy said, lifting his eyebrows. "I made sure to let them know how helpful you were to the investigation."

Noah's shoulders eased up and he smiled as

Randy exited the room.

"What was *that* about?" Molly asked after Noah settled beside her on the bed.

"Nothing," he said. "Just an understanding between us."

"So, your parents weren't mad about you sneaking out last night?"

"No. According to your dad, I *didn't* sneak out last night. I came to your rescue at a very crucial point of an investigation. He told them I was a hero," he said, proudly.

That's when Molly decided Noah *had* been a hero last night. To her. But, she was too embarrassed to tell him to his face. Instead, she kept it to herself with the hope that maybe, just maybe Noah already knew.

When it came time to show him the money, Molly pulled the whole wad out of the box and shoved it in his face. Noah's eyes went wide when she told him the total amount, and how it was actually contraband that needed a good hiding place.

"Do you even know what *contraband* even means?" Noah asked, rolling his eyes.

Molly was offended. "Not by definition," she said. "But I *do* know that I used it correctly in my sentence, which is all that really matters."

Noah seemed to give up at that. "Well, I

happen to know the perfect place to hide the money," he said, standing up.

"You do?"

He nodded. "But you'll need your firefly jar. You still have it, right?"

Molly stood up, wondering where it was. She spun around, trying to find it, wondering where her dad would have put it. "Help me find it, Noah," she said as they pulled up her covers and peeked under her bed.

But it wasn't there...or anywhere.

"That's strange. I'm sure he wouldn't have left it in the car..."

"Molly," Noah said.

She turned around.

He was standing inside Molly's closet with the door opened just a crack. She peeked in. On the top shelf above her clothes was the firefly jar, tucked inside the shoebox filled with her mother's old things, the shoebox Molly had purposely shoved into the back of the closet so she wouldn't have to think about it anymore...

So, what was the firefly jar doing in here?

Noah handed Molly the box. She sat on her bed and opened it up. The stack of Tom Flaky's old, yellowed photos seemed to fit nicely inside the box beside the newer photos—the ones of Molly and her mother together.

Mom.

Molly glanced again at the firefly jar still flickering with light, though the golden hue had faded some. She tipped it sideways for a better view, noticing that two of the fireflies had already died; their lifeless, lightless bodies were lying upside down at the bottom of the jar. Dead.

Dead.

Molly lowered the jar and grabbed Tom's note, re-reading his riddle more carefully.

1. Fireflies can only live in a warm, humid environment (or a pseudo-environment created for them inside a jar).

HOWEVER,

2. Fireflies can only live in a jar for a few days.

A few days. If that.

Molly glanced up at Noah, who stood silently beside her, waiting.

"I found the firefly jar," she said, even though she knew he was the one who'd found it for her. "Now, show me that perfect hiding place."

His eyes crinkled and his mouth spread wide into a smile. "Follow me," he said, walking out the door.

This time, Molly had figured the riddle out all by herself.

CHAPTER
35
An Impossible Wish

Noah and Molly dangled their feet over the open crawl space trapdoor. The earthy aroma of cool, damp underground filled the closet. Molly turned to Noah, offering him another cinnamon bear. She was already on her third.

"I'm pretty sure being at Bell's Bluff in the middle of the night is a lot more terrifying than this," she said, biting into another bear, loving how the sweet burn ignited in her mouth like fire.

Noah held onto the rusted metal box and jumped down into the hole. His head poked above the ground. "You're exactly right," he said, ducking beneath the floor. "That's why this is going to be a piece of cake."

"So, why do it?"

"Close the door."

"What? Now? Don't you want the firefly jar, first?"

"Nope. No help this time. But I still need you to count for me just in case I count too fast or slow."

"Fine. Whatever. But, just because you cross this off your list doesn't make you any more macho. You understand that, right? There are a lot of idiotic things kids do that sound brave, like riding skateboards off of roofs or catching themselves on fire."

"Are you telling me you think I'm an idiot?"

"Well...no. I just want to make it clear that I think your list is pointless."

"Well, it's my list, not yours. So why does it matter? Just close the door and start counting, and remember, don't open it until you've gotten to one hundred and twenty. Got it?"

"Sure," Molly said, dropping the trapdoor shut just as Noah's head disappeared beneath the floor.

Surprisingly, after counting to one hundred and twenty, Noah had still not returned. Molly pulled the door open and poked her head down into the black hole, looking for any sign of Noah.

It seemed he had disappeared.

"Hellooo?" she called. "It's way past one-twenty now, and I'm getting sick of holding up the door. Noah?"

Molly waited.

Silence.

And then, "Molly, you've got to come down here and see this!"

"What? There is no way I'm going down there. This is *your* list, not mine."

More silence.

"Hello?" Molly called.

"I'm serious. Check it out."

Molly waited, wondering if Noah was playing some kind of joke on her, trying to lure her into falling for some dirty, disgusting under-the-house trick. But then she realized Noah didn't play dumb tricks like that. He actually seemed intrigued by something, and pretty soon Molly was more curious than disgusted by the possibility of skeletons and spiders crawling around. Mostly because Noah wasn't much for exaggerating.

"Okay, fine," she agreed. "But if I feel one creepy thing crawling on me, you're dead, do you understand?"

"Close the door. And leave the fireflies up there. You can see it much better when it's pitch black."

Pitch black. Not Molly's favorite description for dark, but she supposed after last night she'd seen worse.

Once the door was shut, Molly dropped to her hands and knees and crawled toward the sound of Noah's voice, totally getting why it was called a crawl space.

"What do you want?" she demanded after finally reaching him.

"Turn around, on your back," he ordered.

"Seriously?"

"Just do it. Please. You're already down here."

"Fine. But this better be worth—"

And then she saw it—a personalized message written in glow-in-the-dark paint on the underside of the floorboards, just for Noah.

**I KNEW YOU COULD DO IT, NOAH.
I'VE ALWAYS KNOWN YOU WERE BRAVE.**

"No way!" Molly exclaimed, staring at the glowing letters. "It's for you! How cool is that?" she yelled, grabbing onto his arm.

He didn't say anything, but kept sniffling like his allergies had gotten the best of him. But Molly knew Noah didn't have allergies.

"Who's it from?" she asked. "Your mom?"

"No. This one's from my dad," he said, sniffing again.

They remained under the house together for another one hundred and twenty seconds until Noah got his allergies under control. Then she told him not to move because she had one more thing she needed to get.

Molly crawled her way back through the dark, still not loving the dirt and stench of underground all around her, but grateful nothing alive had attacked her...yet.

When she found the square of light peeking through the trapdoor, she stood and pushed it open, popping her head above the floor to look for the one thing she still needed to take care of.

The firefly jar.

She pulled it down into the dark with her and followed its light back to Noah. He was now leaning against the foundation wall with his hands resting on his knees.

He looked so perfect, just sitting in the dark like that with nothing to be afraid of. She thought of the past twenty-four hours, how Noah had been there for her no matter what, even when faced with the possibility of groundation, and things far worse than the wrath of his parents.

Tom Flaky had been right. Noah *was* a loyal friend.

And Molly was lucky to have him.

When she reached him, she couldn't help herself. She threw her arms around him, unable to contain her emotions from not only the last few days...but also since...

Since her mother died.

There, she said it.

Molly's mother died, and there was nothing she could do about it. There was nothing her dad could do about it. There was nothing the doctors could do about it. Molly had always known it was the truth, but it was much easier blaming somebody else than letting that blame float out in the open, just wandering around aimlessly with no place to land.

Like a firefly.

Noah's arms around her were gentle, and he seemed to understand what this was all about, even if he didn't have a response.

Molly finally pulled away from him. "Thanks, Noah."

"For what? I'm the one that dragged you down here."

"No. Not for *this*. For...*everything else*. For climbing up Candlestick Hill with me even when you didn't want to. For deciphering clues and for coming with me on the Night Train and the carnival, and cheering me up when I was scared...and for the Ferris wheel ride...and...and...

She couldn't think of anything else.

"Wow," he mumbled, embarrassed.

Molly hadn't meant to make such a scene.

Noah clasped his hands together, and the firefly jar lit up the space in between them as they sat there in awkward silence.

She felt stupid now.

"I finally thought of my wish," Molly said, hoping to get things back to normal.

"What wish?" he asked.

"For the firefly jar. Remember what the firefly man said? That I had to make a perfect wish?"

Noah smiled. "That's right. You couldn't even think up a single wish."

She elbowed him and he turned his head, his eyes catching hers. "Yes, I could. I just didn't want to make it. Not yet."

"Oh yeah? What is it?"

"It's a *wish*, remember? I'm not supposed to say it out loud."

Noah rolled his eyes. "You're not exactly a role model for following rules, don't you think? Come on...I'm really curious now. What is it?"

"It's much *better* than a birthday wish, that's what it is."

"I know. I can already tell by the look on your face."

"It's a wish that can't ever come true."

"How do you know it can't come true?"

"I just know."

He straightened his legs and leaned back on his hands. "Then why wish for it?" he asked, watching her.

"You're the one who said it first. At the carnival."

"Said what?"

"That real wishes shouldn't be easy."

"Oh, right. I guess I remember saying something like that."

"Wishes should be made of the impossible, the outrageous, the unbelievable, don't you think?" Molly said, thinking of the Night Train, thinking of the Midnight Carnival and the fireflies in her jar that, no matter what she did or how long she waited, would all eventually die.

That was the answer to Tom's firefly riddle—that Molly couldn't save the fireflies. Whether she kept them safe inside the jar, or opened the lid and let them go—either way they would die because Blue Rock Island was not warm or humid. Her home wasn't good for fireflies at all.

But, fireflies weren't meant to stay in a jar.

The thought came to her after looking at all her mother's old jewelry and pictures—wouldn't it be better to let the fireflies go, and light up the world on their way out?

That's what Molly needed to do—to set the memory of her mother free for the world to see, rather than keeping her all cooped up inside her heart for only Molly to feel.

Molly leaned over and whispered her very best wish into Noah's ear.

He seemed to give it some thought, and then turned his head until their eyes were matched up and Molly nearly got lost inside those dark circles lit up by firefly light.

"Perfect," he said, smiling. "It's an absolutely *perfect* wish—one the firefly man would approve of, I bet."

At the very back corner of the crawlspace beneath the house, two feet away from the spot where Noah hid the rusted metal box containing a wad of hundred dollar bills for safekeeping, Molly raised the firefly jar and unscrewed the metal lid.

One by one the fireflies found their way out—some in dizzying spurts and others in drunken zigzags, and even a few straight up and out like they knew exactly where they were going and what they wanted to do with their freedom.

Molly's heart, a twisting, confusing mess of sadness and excitement and love felt extra full as she watched each firefly slowly drift away.

Then, she released out loud to the world a perfect, impossible wish: "I wish you were here with me, Mom."

Even though she knew her wish would never come true, not even in a million years. Yet, Molly still wished it *because she could.*

Because she knew that wishing for the impossible was better than never wishing at all.

EPILOGUE

Molly looked out the window at the thick cloud of grey floating outside, hoping the blue might be strong enough to break through before the end of the day. It was September third, which meant school started in one week.

Frank Sinatra was singing in the background, this time not about *flying away* but something about having the world on a string. Molly liked the sound of that—*I've got the world on a string sitting on a rainbow, got the string around my finger...*

It made her happy.

Her hands were a mess, covered in flour dust and bits of dried-up dough. She loved the way the business of doughnut making made her hands feel—*important*. After the giant-sized mixer kneaded the dough, Randy Pepper hefted the steel bowl up in his arms and dumped the mound of dough onto the counter. Together, he and Molly pushed and stretched the dough until it was flat enough to work the rolling pin back and forth across it.

Next, Molly ran the big rolling pin fitted with a dozen doughnut cutters over the dough—and like magic, forty doughnuts were cut, all ready to be scooped up and set on a tray to rise.

But, that was the point at which Molly's dad took over. Because when the doughnuts were done rising, they were ready for frying, and Randy wasn't willing to let his daughter accidentally fry her fingers yet, at least not until she was eighteen.

Molly thought it considerate of him.

After washing up at the sink, she tidied up the front of the store before the first customers would start arriving. Molly had a hard time believing she'd been awake for two hours now, even though it was not quite 8 am. But, she much preferred this arrangement, working side by side with her dad instead of being left alone all night and her dad sleeping all day.

Of course, that would all change once school started...but at least she'd still have her dad all to herself at night.

Officer Wolfe and Ruby Dodd disappeared from Blue Rock Island after their final encounter at the top of Candlestick Hill, along with the faded blue car with its old-fashioned wheels. Molly was almost positive a black mini cooper had showed up in its place, but Officer Pepper told her to ignore it.

Still, they could never be too sure.

So, the wad of hundred dollar bills remained hidden inside the rusted metal box for another month, until late July, when Randy finally sent Noah back under the house to retrieve the box. Noah gladly obliged, now that he was no longer afraid of small dark spaces. He'd since moved on to goal number 4, though he refused to tell Molly just what that entailed, claiming his entire life did not need to be an open book to her.

Molly decided that made sense, and finally quit bugging him about it.

From the eight thousand dollars they took six thousand, five hundred of it to the bank and bought *Flaky's Fantastic Doughnuts*. Molly had convinced her dad he was already so good at working graveyard as a policeman, that he'd be even better at making doughnuts. Plus, after the whole incident with the FBI on June 13th, Randy Pepper was on the lookout for a new job.

The rest of the money, Randy said, would be put away for Molly's future.

But, for now, Molly's future remained secure by her dad's side behind the counter of *Flaky's*

Fantastic Doughnuts. This morning, as she carried two trays loaded with an array of glossy, colored doughnuts to the front counter, the front door opened to the sound of footsteps tapping along the tile toward the counter.

"I'll be with you in a minute," Molly said, her head buried inside the glass case as she transferred the doughnuts one by one from the tray into the case.

"Take your time," said a man with a southern accent.

"Do you know what you want?" Molly asked, her head still stuffed inside the case.

"I think I'm in the mood for a fritter. Are those ready yet?"

The man sounded so cheerful for such a drab morning, and Molly wondered where he was from. Southern accents were rare around the bay area.

"No. Those still need about thirty more minutes," she said.

"No problem at all. I can wait."

Okay, Molly thought, wondering what the man was going to do for thirty minutes. Hopefully not bug her—she had work to do.

After the doughnuts were perfectly lined up inside the case, Molly stood up to admire her work, and then glanced over the counter at her first customer of the day. The man with the southern accent was sitting at a table in the corner, his back to the wall and a newspaper spread open in front of him.

"Wow. Did you see this?" he said loud enough for Molly to hear. She thought he was talking to somebody on his phone, so she remained silent.

The man flipped down the upper corner of his newspaper, revealing the top of his face. He wore glasses and had a thick red beard, and a plaid beret rested atop his head.

"What? Are you talking to me?" Molly asked, surprised when he looked at her directly.

"Yes."

"Oh. Sorry," she said, wondering why this man was even talking to her.

The man scooted forward in his seat and lowered the paper even more. Then he pointed to the bottom of the front page. Molly couldn't read the words from where she stood, but could clearly make out the bold, black and white illustration of a train.

Her attention was piqued. She stepped around the counter.

"It looks like the Night Train is back," the man said.

Molly froze. "What? Are you sure?"

"Says so right here. Take a look." He dropped the paper on the table and turned it toward Molly as she approached. Sure enough, at the very bottom quarter of the newspaper was an ad announcing the return of the Night Train.

Molly stepped back from the table and jumped up and down. "He's back! He's back! He's back!"

But then she stopped and covered her mouth after realizing what she'd just said. *Out Loud.* It was easy to forget that there were certain things she was never allowed to say out loud. And any mention of Molly's grandfather was one of those things.

"Not a word," her Dad had instructed her the day after Tom disappeared. "No matter what." Because they didn't ever want to spoil the remote chance that maybe, just maybe Molly's grandfather might come back.

The newspaper blew off the table and floated to the ground as the front door of the shop slowly closed inward. Molly looked up to find her dad staring at her from the back room, giving her a look of caution.

She turned back to her customer, ready to make up some kind of reason for her outburst. But he was gone.

Like he'd vanished.

Vanished into thin air without his fritter.

———

Later that afternoon, after closing the shop for the day, Molly found a nice napping spot on the back patio in a hammock while her dad camped out in front of the TV for a Giants game.

The sun played peek-a-boo through the fog as she waited for Noah to arrive. Molly's dad had given her the okay to tell Noah about the Night Train ad, as long as she kept it to straight talk about what was in the paper. No speculating, no mentioning Tom Flaky's name or anything that might lead the FBI to believe Tom had anything to do with the Night Train. *If* they were even still listening.

Chances were the FBI was following some other lead Tom had already distracted them with. He was good at distractions.

"Hey," said Noah, rounding the corner.

Molly sat up, excited to see him. "It's back!" she said with a grin, getting right to the point.

"*What's* back?" Noah asked, holding his hands behind his back.

"Hey, what's behind your back?" Molly pointed, trying to peek around his torso. But he kept turning just enough to prevent whatever he was holding from being seen.

"Noah, stop it!" Molly yelled, jumping out of the hammock and pulling at his arm. "What are you hiding?"

"*What's back?*" Noah repeated, pushing Molly away. "You sounded excited on the phone. First tell me what you're talking about, and then I'll show you."

"Promise?"

"Promise."

Her eyes lit up as she told him about the Night Train.

Noah smiled, though not a smile bursting with excitement. This one was different. This was a smile that knew something big and couldn't wait to tell what it was.

Molly waited for him to reveal whatever it was.

Through his smile, he finally said, "I *know*."

"*You know?*" she asked, deflated. "How do you *know*? You suddenly read the paper now?"

He shook his head. "Nope."

"Then, how do you already know about the Night Train?"

"Because the UPS man just gave me this envelope," he said, finally bringing his hands out from behind his back.

"He gave *you* an envelope? What for?" Molly asked, wondering what a UPS delivery had to do with Noah's perpetual smile.

"He probably knew more about what's inside this letter than he did about being a deliveryman," Noah said, handing Molly a crème-colored envelope with her name printed on the front.

Molly's heart soared inside, and she couldn't stop smiling. *"Was it him?"* she asked, wanting to jump up and down.

"I don't know."

"What did he look like?"

"Brown shirt, brown shorts."

"Noah! Tell me!"

"I don't know! I wasn't really paying attention." But Noah was still smiling.

"Come on," Molly whispered. "*Tell me.* Did he have the number 13 tattooed on his finger?"

Noah exhaled and looked both ways. A streak of sunlight cut through an opening in the fog, and Noah pulled Molly onto the hammock with him.

As they swung back and forth, he admitted, "I didn't look at his hands."

Molly's heart sank, until Noah started talking again. "But, he was bald like the Englishman, and his voice was raspy like the firefly man, and he had a dark, handlebar moustache like the Ferris Wheel operator, and, and..."

"And what?" Molly asked, trying to picture it all in her head. She wanted to leap off the hammock and shout out loud, but held it all in, just in case.

"And he had deep blue eyes...just like..."

Molly closed her eyes, waiting for the final

description. "Just like who, Noah…?" she asked quietly.

"Just like your grandpa," he whispered in her ear.

Molly opened her eyes and smiled, knowing her mother's love was still alive, even if she wasn't, through everyone who cared about her.

And that her mother's love was *real*.

As real as the Night Train.

ACKNOWLEDGMENTS

I owe the initial inspiration for Molly Pepper's adventures to my dad and his short career as a small-town policeman. He would often surprise us with midnight trips to Flaky's Cream Doughnuts to watch the doughnuts come to life after choosing any doughnut we wanted in the entire store! There, we also met other cops working the graveyard shift, and like Molly, I usually chose the apple fritter because it was the biggest and most delicious. Thank you, Mom and Dad and the cute perfect town of Walnut Creek for a childhood filled with innocence that allowed my imagination to flourish. Thank you Kristin, Justin and Caroline and my neighborhood friends Ceci, Ginger, and Danny for our adventures (even if I did have to be Darth Vader because of my boy haircut).

247

Thank you to my wonderful, supportive, beautiful and brilliant critique partners Ella Olsen and Bobi Gehret. Thank you to my littlest creation Kate Walker for being my very first target-age reader, and for staying up late to read before offering me spot-on suggestions in the morning. Thank you, Andrew, for loving whatever I do no matter what. Thank you to Brett and Elizabeth for keeping me on my toes and supporting me even though you both hate to read and write (*sob!*). And to my always supportive and sweet and patient husband, Greg, for loving me exactly how I am. I love you.

And lastly, thank you to Lisa Paul for always believing in me and my stories and for seeing the good in everything, and to Dawn Sloane-Doerr and Lands Atlantic Publishing for your critical eye, for all your efforts in bringing *Molly Pepper and the Night Train* to life.

ALSO *BY*

COURTNEY KING WALKER!

A wonderful, touching Young Adult debut!

Visit www.courtneykingwalker.com

MORE FROM

LANDS ATLANTIC PUBLISHING:

If you liked Molly Pepper, try meeting Lucas Cage in this clever adventure as he gets himself out of trouble!

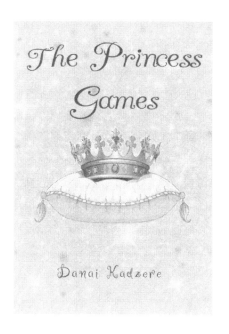

The king and queen need a princess,
and they need her fast! Feel free to sit in
while Emma competes in The Princess
Games!

CPSIA information can be obtained
at www.ICGtesting.com
Printed in the USA
FSOW02n1829260815
10175FS

9 780985 725051